CATCHING
MICE

CATCHING MICE

A Novel

HADYN J. ADAMS

不管是白猫还是黑猫，抓到老鼠的就是好猫

authorHOUSE®

AuthorHouse™
1663 Liberty Drive
Bloomington, IN 47403
www.authorhouse.com
Phone: 1-800-839-8640

Published by AuthorHouse   09/07/2012

ISBN: 978-1-4772-2264-5 (sc)
ISBN: 978-1-4772-2263-8 (e)

不管是白猫还是黑猫，抓到老鼠的就是好猫

It doesn't matter whether a cat is black or white as long as it catches mice.

[Deng Xiao Ping 1904-1997]

This book is dedicated to

Aravind Adiga for giving me a great read in his novel, *The White Tiger,* and that gave rise to the idea for this one

And to

My many wonderful friends in China

And to

The People's Republic of China—a great country and a great nation!

By the same author

Ecstatic from One Lie

Published by Author House : 2012

Mr Wen Jiabao is a man of the people and as such has instructed me to reply on his behalf and that of The People's Republic of China. With his permission, therefore, I have instructed a representative cross-section of citizens of China today to write their brief biographies and their comments on the state of the nation in the 21st century and that should give you an insight into the 'real' China just as you have so kindly given us a snapshot of India or at least of entrepreneurial India as you see it. The persons who have been selected are :-

Mr Wu Dabin : School Maintenance Engineer from Anhui Province, living and working in Shanghai.

Mrs Jiang Shulin : (Mr Wu's wife—don't be put off by the different name, that's the way it is in China): Ayi from Anhui province, living and working in Shanghai.

Ms Fu Langong : Social Services, from Changzhou, Jiangsu Province, living and working in Shanghai.

Ms Jenny Jing : Company Project Developer from Beijing, living and working in Beijing.

Ms Michelle Wong : Restaurant, bar and club owner from Hong Kong, living and working in Beijing

Peter Zhang : son of the millionaire, David Zhang, from Beijing. Living (but hardly working!) in Beijing.

So that you get the bigger picture, we have also included a write-up from an ex-pat :-

Bill Fowler : Company Director, from Manchester, UK, living and working in Shanghai and all places south and west!

I have taken the trouble of getting their submissions (other than Bill Fowler's that is) translated into English—mind you, his vocabulary and syntax could do with a bit of improvement—which I know you can read and write.

I hope you see that China is the land of opportunity, just like India, but that it is not necessary to murder anyone to achieve success here. (Having said that people are murdered here but for not for reasons of personal advancement of course!)

I hope you enjoy reading the stories of our comrades and the ex-pat . . . . oh, and by the way, you lucky bugger, this is the totally unexpurgated version which is certainly not available in mainland China* and if it were known I sent you this edition, I would be murdered!

Yours sincerely
Sheng Yapin
(Secretary)

*Well, it may be available at The Bookworm in Sanlitun, Beijing, or maybe even in the Chengdu habitat which goes by the same name—we have ways of knowing there's not much they don't have by way of banned works there.

BILL

"I have almost a feminine partiality for old china." Oh, forget that! Just me being pretentious and remembering crap I read in my school days. Check the quote out on Google. I love China : modern China, the country that is, not bits of porcelain! In fact, ever since I first got here in 1996 I have fallen in love with this great country. Hey and I've been lucky enough to live in Beijing and Shanghai and all places south and west!

So I've been domiciled here for the best part of 16 years : can't speak a word of the language. Well, that's not quite true—I get by on taxi driver's Chinese—well all us ex-pats know that because the stupid bastards here don't have 'the knowledge'. They expect you to know where you're going and more often than not how to get there. So you have to learn *you guai, zuo guai, yizhi chaoqian* and if you're really advanced *hong lu deng, shizi lukou* as well as the names of the places/roads you want to arrive at. You'd think being neighbours to Japan they'd all have 'sat nav' but when you think about it that wouldn't be much good here since roads appear and disappear just like buildings in Shanghai, Beijing and all places south and west whenever your back is turned! Like spaghetti junction in Brum? Don't make me laugh! With all the elevated highways and what have you here this place is one massive noodle junction! Well, it may be grey, uninviting chaos during the day but it all looks good lit up in its fairy lights at night as you can see on the postcards they sell! Mind you, there's one good thing about the drivers here and that is they can all read their own language so even if you cannot say Portman using three syllables and not two they will be able to read if you can get a native (probably an hotel receptionist or your P.A.) to write it down for them. Failing that, get a company/business card (usually in English one side, Chinese the other)—they just love those—and show it to the driver (right side round, mind you!) and you should be OK.

Well that's how you normally get around in this country without being bilingual . . . . but it's not how you get by . . . . but I'll fill you in on that later.

I first came here, as I said, in 1996. I was seconded by the university I was then working for to Wuxi to work and liaise with Jiangnan University and Wuxi University of Light Industry. (I've a degree in Chemistry and am a specialist in materials analysis. I've since changed tack from the realms of academe as you will see!) Strange name that for a university—I guess UMIST is our nearest equivalent though I've often speculated that since the act of incorporation perhaps we should have had a City University of Newcastle upon Tyne as the acronym of that would sum up the standards of the new "punyversities" (as I like to call them!) Oh, and by the way, here they also have what they call 'normal' universities (actually these are mainly teacher training establishments) but it makes you think what the abnormal ones must be like!

Things were different back in 1996 (but not as different as they would have been in the 70's and 80's)! Wuxi, being close to Shanghai, was a kind of mini Shanghai with its factories and businesses and its city development but with a very rural churlishness in its population. Used to get stared at in the street, a kind of evil eye, when I was out and about and the market place—now replaced by a glitzy but tacky shopping mall complete with bubbling stream, gushing fountains and rainbow lights as well as the de-rigeur Starbucks (where you can buy a Wuxi City mug!)—was a place of blood, sweat and tears. Not a place to frequent if you were squeamish or loved animals! Blood spattered here there and everywhere from the chickens (from their Rooster Coop!) and other animals and fish being slaughtered, sweat from the market vendors piling crate upon crate full of gargantuan sized fruit (not many of them to the pound as the smutty sea-side postcards would say!) and veg that would have won copious prizes in any rural Autumn Fayre in the UK and tears from ex-pats like me being ripped off having to pay four or five times the local price for anything and everything . . . . though, mind you, it was still cheap at those prices and so very, very fresh . . . . even though you were paying for some serious lumps of earth which had refused to disengage themselves from the vegetables until they had to be hosed off in your sink at home.

Used to be good in the restaurants as well. "No good going into them places. You don't know what you're eating." Thus my father dismissing the burgeoning growth of Chinese restaurants in the U K in the sixties and after. Why he should have been so critical I will never know, though perhaps he was typical of his generation. After all, eating out during the war could seriously damage your health especially during air-raids. And then again, the working class didn't exactly have a restaurant culture. Yet, as a died-in-the-wool smoker—*Players* untipped always—and quite a good spitter and throat clearer, he clearly had two attributes at least which would have endeared him to this society. But no. Wouldn't go near them. "You don't know what you're eating."

It is easy to criticise our progenitors. The clash of age and youth in all its many facets is too big a subject for this book—maybe next time round? We, the carefree, golden, sexually liberated youth of the sixties hit those Chinese restaurants like they offered the best thing since sliced bread (which my father also denounced!)—well, they did, didn't they? We had our *Little Red Books* and we were going to boost that Chinese Cultural Revolution by giving these places our custom, too thick—we were all university students after all—to realise that the restaurant owners were the lucky defectors from that revolution. Sweet and sour pork! Yummy. Rice! Great! Sweet and sour chicken! Yummy! Rice! Great! Sweet and sour . . . . However, it is interesting to note, that more often than not, our parents were right—God, how we hate to admit that!—or nearly right most of the time. In this case I grudgingly must admit my father was nearly right. Yes nearly right. What he should have said was not, "You don't know what you are eating," but "You don't want to know what you are eating."

Now, the big scandal in the U K during the growth of the Chinese Restaurant market was that they cooked dog. Yes! Dog! Ugh! How could they . . . .? I mean, man's best friend and all that! (Only ex-pat Egyptians seemed to spread rumours about them also eating cats—no one took much notice of the Egyptians, of course. How ridiculous! Cats indeed? I ask you!) Anyway, stories abounded of police raids and seizures of meat which turned out to be dog. Prosecutions followed. Restaurants were temporarily closed. Yes! Dog! How could they . . . .? Disgusting! What a laugh! Dog? Just dog? Yeah, just dog! Have you looked at a menu in a Chinese restaurant in China? O.K. So I accept you can't read it. Fine. No need. Have a walk around the restaurant. Recognise any of the fish in the tanks? Are there really prawns that big? Getaway, that's not a squid! Wow, that snake looks colourful! Wow, that snake looks big! Oh, what a beautiful Portuguese Man o' War—you don't see them very often, do you? Well, I've never seen black and red chickens before! Or black ducks, come to that. Local, obviously. Oh those bulbous frogs—like something out of Jurassic Park! (They actually call them XXX large paddy-field chickens—a good translation). Ah, a hedgehog? Hmmmm. And we? We were worried about dog! Dog . . . . delicious! No problem! Sweet and sour with rice that is, of course! (Incidentally, how many dogs or cats do you see as pets per head of population in this country? Lock up your pets, not your daughters!) Truth to tell though, a dog has recently started to become a bit of a fashion statement for some families and for young ladies of a certain profession especially in the main cities like Shanghai and Beijing.

Now going to a Chinese restaurant in China with all your mates from home even if it has a menu in English is no way to get to know the local eating scene. After all, none of you is going to order bullfrog, are you? Nor, come to that, since you have an aversion to Chinese dates and walnuts, will you order the sauted rat served with Chinese dates and glazed walnuts. Nor will you order deep fried local insects. So what's the point? You'll stick to the sweet and sour pork! Yummy! Rice! Great! Though one of you may just chance it a little and suggest going for the lemon chicken—very daring! A more adventurous member among you (who may just have done GCSE Biology) may chance it even further and ask for one of the fish that looks a bit like something seen in a picture in one of the U K text books. It's a bit disconcerting to get the said fish netted and brought to you flapping about for your due consideration before the dinner but that's the way it is here. This part is a bit like the wine waiter pouring that itsy bitsy teeny weeny drop of wine into the glass and asking is it O.K. Have you ever said no? Are you going to have the nerve to reject this fish that has just splattered water all over the place and maybe even you? Of course not. After all, you selected to have it. But . . . . .

Twenty minutes (or sometimes even less!) later there is that same fish on the plate before you. Dead. Not flapping around like it was when you casually cast your eyes over it and pronounced its death sentence. Oh, yes! That's what you did. It's now covered in miscellaneous herbs and swimming in soy sauce, not the fish tank. And its eyes—those spaniel eyes are looking accusingly at you. Directly at you. What is it saying?

"You unfeeling, uncaring bastard! Twenty minutes ago I was with my mates having a swim, minding my own business in that big tank up there. O.K., so I wasn't free : but I was bleeding well alive! Alive! Then along you came. Eyed me. Got me netted and wham! Hoiked out of the water and presented to you like the head of John the Baptist to Salome before being taken into the kitchen. You didn't care what happened to me. Like Pontius Pilate you were : "I can find no fault with this fish . . . ." Steamed, I was. Steamed! Steamed! What a way to die! Just you wait until the Grand Master of the Nets comes and trawls you in, squire! I hope it's more than steaming what you get. Know what I mean? . . . ."

At this point, you will either be so overcome with remorse and guilt that you will completely lose your appetite, vow to give everlasting homage to Buddha and become a committed vegan for the rest of your entire life and vote forever for The Green Party. Those spaniel, accusatory eyes will haunt you for evermore and make you keep this promise. Or, you will shrug your shoulders and nonchalantly, casually, dismissively even, grab those chopsticks, dig into that tender, succulent, soft, tasty fishy flesh and guzzle it down and after, just remark, "That's showbusiness!" Yummy!

Well, it used to be like that but things have changed a bit since SARS of course . . . .

PETER

Hi! I'm Peter. Not my real name of course—that's Zhang Xie. What do you say in your country—idle rich? Yeah. I'm one of those. Fucking shit rich to be exact! being one of the many noveau riche in P.R.C.

By the way, you don't mind if I smoke do you? Polite of me to ask really as in China smoking may be supposedly banned in some places but in reality that's a law that is "more honoured in the breach than the observance." I think Shakespeare must have been writing generally about China when he wrote that.

Surprised are you by my erudition? Don't be. Dad—he's fucking loaded—sent me to boarding school in Australia to be educated. Come to think of it, given that scenario maybe you ought to be astonished rather than surprised, that is? What's the difference between a natural yoghurt and an Australian—the former has a culture! Sorry about that!

Oh, would you like a cold tinnie, by the way? No? Don't mind if I do, do you? Thought not.

Ah well, yeah, Dad. He's a land owner. Owns loads of mus (i.e. acres) of land and is also a developer so he can make money twice over . . . . and he has done . . . . and, with a little help from me, continues to do so. I help him spend it, too, of course. I drive a Ferrari and I've also a Mercedes which my bodyguard drives me round in. He's the fatso standing over there with that huge grin on his face. He always has that huge grin even when he's doing someone over who has been bothering me. You know the type—keeps on and on and even when you say, "Wo shuo bu nandao ni ting bu dong ma" (What part of the word *no* don't you understand?) keeps going like a record stuck in the grove—or should that be a CD or a DVD?

I, or should I say we, that's Mum, Dad and me and my occasional family—more of that later—live on the outskirts of Beijing—within easy access of the ji chang gao su (Airport Express way) of course—can't miss out on the city life. Dad, when he worked for the government in the past, travelled extensively in Europe and fell in love with the architecture of the west—God knows why as Chinese traditional architecture is just as appealing! (Having said that, all our Olympic venues and new buildings in Beijing seem to have been designed by fucking foreigners!) Anyway, having made all his dosh he used it to build an exact, well almost exact, replica of Neuschwanstein Castle in Germany. That was built by Mad King Ludwig; ours was built by my mad father. People drive out this way just to stare at it. I guess they do a double-take . . . . Am I in China? Am I in Germany? Where the fuck am I? Confused and confusing. Damn clever these Chinese!

Actually it's so big we only live in a wing of it and the rest doubles as a hotel—not a very successful one—don't reckon we get even 20% occupancy in hotel client terms on an annual average but, boy do we do well when they want a venue for local government cadre training (well, Dad still has his contacts!) and we do even better for weddings. Oh and we did host part of the Russian delegation when they came over for the Olympics. But, yeah, it's great as a backdrop for the local shelias when they get hitched. Well, it's Disneyland stuff for them, isn't it? Yeah, the marriage is as well—all a romantic dream that fades eventually. Not that our wonderland castle fades though the extremes of climate of this capital don't do the building any favours. Don't look too closely, inside or out : Chinese aren't noted for putting in damp courses that work and we do have a reputation for not observing intellectual property rights and that applies to materials used even in construction. I guess if we were going to sell it we'd have to go to the Yashow Market.

Ah, I note that reference is lost on you. Well, as I was saying, we do have a reputation for not observing intellectual property rights . . . .

FU

C all me Fiona!

Being born and brought up in Changzhou was no picnic I can tell you especially as me and my twin sister were born in 1974 and the Cultural Revolution may have been on its last legs but those legs were still pretty strong. Chairman Mao (PBUH—oops that's a Muslim addition for Mohammed, isn't it?—Learned that from .... oh, maybe I'll tell you later) was also on his last legs (or maybe more off than on them given his medical condition)—only just that is, but he was alive (even if he wasn't kicking) and that meant the country suffered because he suffered .... or was it because Jiang Jing suffered or was mad? Perhaps because K'ang Sheng had died and her old man was heading for the great politburo up above—the sky is red sometimes!—and therefore she wasn't getting enough? No one seems to care so much now as they did back then but suffer we did, I'm telling you. We had an elder sister as well. Dad worked on the railways, when they were running that is! Mum was a traditional Chinese housewife. Five in the family and then there was Granfa and Granma . . . .

I don't want to say life was hard but being a twin I (and my sister) only got half the hand-me-downs each from our older sister. And don't believe those that say half a loaf is better than none—that's bollocks!—trying living on our equivalent of half a half of loaf! The railways didn't pay all that much, and especially so when they weren't running from time to time though the great survivor, good old Deng Xiaoping (PBUH—I really wish could get out of that habit!) did turn that around eventually and look at the super service we have nationwide now! High speed, luxury trains . . . . the lot! My dad's retired now, of course, and that helps account for things as well. So most of the time back then all we could afford were vegetables so we lived a bit like Buddhists. Not that we were Buddhists. Mei Banfa! ("No way" to you!) No not even in Changzhou where there's a big Buddhist monastery—about all there is of interest and that's not really worth visiting. But Jiangsu Province is a bit like Kent—oh, yes, I know about the UK having been there a couple of times but then I have also been to Singapore, The Phillipines, Hong Kong, Thailand, Bali, Italy . . . . more of all that later—the garden of England, so we'd get enough to eat even if we were meat deprived. That's besides the odd paddy-field chicken we caught out in the long grass by the swamps where we used to play on summer evenings—the murmurous haunt of mosquitoes on summer eves!

School, tuition that is, was dull and boring though we all had lots of class mates which is natural when there's 60+ students per class. Didn't do too badly and actually did get into University, though not a good one, to study engineering. But where was that going to get me in the 90s? Sure, China was opening up but a basic education and a crap degree or at least a degree from a crap university was hardly going to take me away from the small world of Changzhou with its Buddhist monastery and its . . . . whatever!

But down the road or at least down the railway line—infrastructure for road transport has only recently become a priority—there was the lure of the big city . . . . Shanghai! Shanghai! So good they named it twice!? Its streets were paved with gold. It was the city of opportunity. There was the Dōngfāng Míngzhūtǎ (Pearl Tower to you) just being built later to be followed by Jīn Mào Dàshà (literally "Golden Prosperity Building to you). What temptation! And I can resist anything except temptation. And yes, I know that's a quote from Oscar Wilde and I know lots of quotes from your famous authors and I'll let you know how and why later . . . .

Well, I had to make it to the big city and amazingly enough me and my friend, Yin Ling, (Annie is the English name she gave herself) got jobs with China Telecom and were sent to Shanghai to train . . . . by train. The training was good but the pay was bad and we had to share a pokey 7 x 7 square metre apartment with toilet, washing and cooking facilities along the corridor and used by 7 other families—how many were in each family I have no idea to this day but you can guess a figure and multiply by it just to see what kind of rabbit warren we were actually in on our floor. On top of that we had a 40 minute metro journey to and from work each day which was added to by a bus journey of 40 minutes to and from the metro to our pokey apartment not to mention a 10-15 minute walk down the street to and from the bus stop—not nice in wet or humid weather which is a feature of Shanghai's climate. We had to get up around 5.30a.m.and never got back until around 8.30p.m. Two young, and I might add attractive girls in a big city only having time to sleep on weekdays and too cream-crackered (do you like my use of the vernacular/rhyming slang?—bet you're wondering how I know all these phrases!) and yuan-less to do much on weekends. Even had to save up to make it back to see our families on the odd weekend in Changzhou.

So it was that one Friday, tired and a bit forlorn as we were, we met Eleanor on the Metro. Ah yes, Eleanor poor soul. Now doing time for a nasty habit she picked up some time before or was it after we met her? But let's look on her

WU DABIN &
JIANG SHULIN

Greetings from me, Mr Wu and my wife Mrs Jiang. We sincerely thank Sheng Yapin for inviting us to contribute to this document to give you a view of modern China. Thank you, too, obviously to our great leader, Comrade Wen Jiabao, truly a man of the people as is President Hu Jintao. We are truly blessed in this country with such excellent leaders who really care for their people and are always putting our good before their own good. Long live The People's Republic of China and the proletariat revolution! Power to the people. The East is Red . . . . (Have I said enough to show I am good, loyal citizen?)

We have recently been told about the scandals of the government of the United Kingdom where it is absolutely clear that those leaders care more about themselves than the people they govern. That is sad. I am sure they can learn from China and our great leaders. After all, we are an enlightened people and country with over 5,000 years of history and we invented Confusianism, Beijing, the Olympics, Mao Zedong thought, paper, writing, fire, roast pork, karaoke, fireworks and chopsticks and I don't know what else but certainly things that have greatly enhanced the existence of mankind throughout the world.

Mrs Jiang is my lovely wife and mother of my son and daughter. My son and daughter do not live with us here in Shanghai where we live and work but they are looked after by my parents, their grandparents, in our home town, Tongling, in Anhui province where they attend the excellently run state schools. It's not far away and they come to visit us and we go to visit them when we can. There is no problem in them living with my parents, their grandparents. We have a great tradition of family life and solidarity in China and always have had and I beg you do not believe people who say this is declining and the divorce rate etc is growing. Please remember we are a great nation of 1.3 billion people (at the last count) and everything has to be seen in perspective. So, a few marriages break up? It's no big deal in such a big population : indeed, it's hardly surprising is it? For most of the time all of us live in a truly harmonious society.

Well, anyway, our marriage, our family is firm as a rock.

Mrs Jiang, she's an ayi. That word is used sometimes as a term of endearment for 'aunt' in China but in this case it is the local vernacular which means she's a skivvy for the rich—usually ex-pats who can't get off their lazy backsides to look after their kids, do their laundry, clean their apartments/houses, do their shopping, walk their dogs or even, in some cases do their cooking would you believe? That's what comes of having a self-indulgent, democratic government, I guess. Anyway, some of her 'employers' are really good to her and treat her well. They are even so kind as to let her have the contents of their fridges and freezers when they piss off on their long holidays back home or to sunny Thailand or to the Maldives or wherever. Lucky bastards! Some of them even let her have the occasional holiday herself—provided she doesn't overdo it and ask for more than the Chinese statutory allowances! Then there's others who try to tell her or rather show her (what a fucking joke!) how to do things—this is the way we wash our dishes, this is the way we scrub our floors, this is the way we polish the silver, this is the way we walk the dog—as if they had been doing it all their lives. I ask you . . . . as if??? Condescending shits that they are! Bloody hell, she's been looking after me and our tribe for the best part of 20 years! Give or take the time our offspring have spent with their grandparents, that is. Do they really think she's that incapable?

However, she's pretty happy about things as she picks up good money from her clients (all cash in hand, of course!) though she does put in the hours—even Saturdays which I grumble about from time to time. She's got her own electric bike now so she gets round the city easily (charges up the battery at the apartments/houses she tends saves on our electricity bills!) and she can afford to treat herself to nice clothes from H & M, Mango or Zara from time to time rather than off the flea markets or the tiny street shops where most things are second hand anyway. Hasn't quite got the income to shop at M & S yet but who knows, she may make enough to get round to that in time. Sometimes she dreams . . . . Gucci, Hermes, Louis Vuitton, Tod's, Fendi, Ferragamo, Dunhill, Paul and Shark—well they've got the biggest stores in Asia here up Nanjing Xi Lu (Nanjing West Road—a bit like London's Oxford Street though my guess it's better than that given your self—indulgent government in the UK). But until we truly realise the Victory of the Proletariat I guess for those sort of goods it's the Yan Xiang market in Pudong where intellectual property rights don't mean the articles the logo is printed on.

Despite all her work with the expats she doesn't speak a word of English and since her employers rarely speak any Chinese communication can be a problem. However, they've now got fridge magnets with English/Mandarin on them so instead of the lazy foreigners doing a bit of language practice other than their taxi-driver's Chinese which would do them good, they just stick the notices on the fridge and expect her to get on with it.

Well, at the moment, that's enough about her. What about me?

Ni hao! Wo shi . . . . Oops, sorry. Wu Dabin—he's my husband. As he's told you I'm an ayi. He's a maintenance man—I guess in your language you'd call him a *Jack of All Trades*—but unlike your guys he is master of them all and has the Chinese certificates to prove it. He works at an international school. There's a lot of them in China now—some are legal, some aren't. Eventually the illegal ones will be closed down but not until someone, somewhere has fleeced the owners sufficiently to get a few foreign holidays and nice retirement home in Canada or Australia.

Actually it was me who got my husband this job. Well, it's women who do most things in this world, don't they? You see I was working as an ayi for Daisy who was the Marketing Manager for one of these schools (a legal one, thank goodness!) and she also got me some work with Mr Harding, the Principal of the school. They are good employers; well, certainly Harding is. He's a nice man : too nice for his own good at times, I reckon. Daisy can be a bit sharp at times but her heart's in the right place. They both are generous to me about holidays (mind you I have to play the mother/daughter in absentia card quite a lot to get this indulgence) and I get the contents of their fridges when they piss off for their long holidays back home or to sunny Thailand or to the Maldives or wherever. Lucky bastards!

Well, Daisy and Harding were setting up this school and I learned they needed some maintenance staff. Oh, yes, in case you're wondering, Daisy speaks Mandarin since she got a scholarship to study at Tsinghua University in Beijing a few years back and she speaks it quite well though her French accent takes a bit of getting used to. So she's my channel of communication and she said she'd talk to Harding about things. He didn't take much convincing but I had to boot my mister Wu Dabin along for an interview with him and Daisy. I guess Daisy did most of the talking then and all my husband did was produce his certificates showing he was, or should I say is, a trained electrician, plumber, builder, surveyor, gas-fitter, painter and decorator, IT and telephone engineer, qualified driver (HGV and PSV), carpenter, cabinet maker, metalworker, car mechanic, swimming pool maintenance manager, masseur etc and he got the job. He's never looked back. From being the one and only maintenance man at the school, since it's grown apace in the last three years he is now head of the maintenance team at the school i.e. he's in charge of 7 other guys who, just like him are all qualified electricians, plumbers, builders, surveyors, gas-fitters, painters and decorators, IT and telephone engineers, qualified drivers (HGV and PSV), carpenters, cabinet makers, metalworkers, car mechanics, swimming pool maintenance managers, masseurs etc. With their experience at the school they are also becoming proficient in English so I wouldn't be at all surprised if they end up as TEFL qualified as well and that will greatly improve their chances of promotion in the future. Oh, yes, China in the 21st century is the land of opportunity, that's for sure thanks to our great leaders, Wen Jiabao and Hu Jintao—not like those in the self-indulgent government of the UK.

So, we are a happily married couple and, as Wu Dabin has said his parents look after our offspring while we work away earning money in the big city of Shanghai. Mind you, I am not altogether happy about his parents looking after my lovely daughter, Dongdong, and my son, Hui (or Gary, that's the English name he has given himself). Wu Dabin's parents can be as dozey as he is at times and for sure, whilst Dongdong is a typical hard-working Chinese girl whom I am sure will get a good gao kao score at her school (and I will make sure she does) Hui has become a bit of a tearaway thanks to their over-indulgence and their constant referral to him as Wu Dabin's "son and heir." I think Hui is taking on western ways, the sort of attitude and behaviour I sometimes see from the students at my husband's school when I go to meet him there. They are encouraged to act like that because of their self-indulgent governments but we have better role models here though sometimes it's hard to convince the likes of Hui about that. If necessary, I may have to go and spend some time with my children so that I can ensure Dongdong's success and get Hui back on the right track. He may not be a great academic like his sister and I don't want to put pressure on him like that, but there's no reason why he can't, like his father, become a qualified electrician, plumber, builder, surveyor, gas-fitter, painter and decorator, IT and telephone engineer, qualified driver (HGV and PSV), carpenter, cabinet maker, metalworker, car mechanic, swimming pool maintenance manager, masseur etc. His English is not good so I don't expect him to get a TEFL qualification, unless that is he gets a job, like his father at an International School. It will be hard to convince him of this as all he thinks about at present is basketball but he's only 5 foot nothing so there's no future in that. Yao Ming has a lot to answer for! "What a fucking joke!" as my husband keeps saying.

I hope that's given you an interesting introduction to us—a fairly typical Chinese family from the countryside (or from what the government euphemistically calls second or indeed third tier cities). The next five year plan of our great government is to bring more education to these cities and especially those inland from the eastern seaboard for now that Shanghai, Tianjin, Qingdao, Dalian, Shenzhen, Zhuhai and the like have almost all completed their face-lifts and are prospering, there's work to be done in Xi'An, Chengdu, Wuhan, Chongqing, Changsha, Kunming etc Well, there's more money to be made and more foreigners to be enticed to invest by the lure of big profits and quick returns—well at least for the Chinese with whom they invest . . . .

PETER

Yashow shichang—Yashow Market, Gongti Bei Lu, Beijing. One of the capital's great tourist attractions. Now it is side by side with Sanlitun Village, a recently built, self-indulgent steel and glass façade of sports and clothes shops and a myriad of restaurants opened just in time for the Olympics. One of the many glass curtains that pervade the city's architectural landscape nowadays. Timing is everything even more than location, location, location, which is just on the opposite side of the street from the famous, or should we say infamous, bar strip? This typifies modern China—the fake next to the real, the good next to the bad. Which is which? It's all a matter of cost—you pays your money and you takes your choice, as they say. Confused and confusing! Damn clever these Chinese!

Well, as I said, if we were going to sell our castle built by my mad father we'd probably have to put it up for sale (or should I say bargaining? or auction?) in Yashow market. We would definitely get a good deal—The Chinese traders always do! Having said that, I never actually went to sell the family folly a couple of years back but did manage to screw a naïve American company out of a few hundred thousand RMB, in cash I might add. Let me tell you the story—it's a homily of what goes on here a lot of the time.

Along comes this group of Americans. "We want to open and international school," they say. "We like your land and the prospect of the fairy tale castle in the background makes the ideal backdrop. Perfect photo opportunity. Would look sensational on the brochure! Can we negotiate? Can you get us a licence?" (Are they selling brochures or a school? I wonder. What were they going to open? A Mickey Mouse school?)

Now I told you my old man (Dad? He's fucking loaded!) owns loads of mus (i.e. acres) surrounding our residence. Some of it was developed for luxury homes—big 5 or 6 bedroomed mansions in their own right either for ex-pats or more often than not for the rich, returning Chinese. The latter coming back from all parts of the globe and bringing with them shed loads of cash from their entrepreneurship in other countries and, of course, crow barring open the floorboards in their former residences which they had restored to them because of their (supposed) suffering and getting the cash, jewellery or whatever else of value they'd hidden there during the Cultural Revolution. Not really nouveau riche—more like old-fashioned aristocrats I guess. Oh, the unpublished stories of the lucky ones during those turbulent years! All you get in the West, perhaps all you want are the sad sob stories of the murdered, abused, imprisoned, violated—you're as much gluttons for punishment as those to whom it was meted out! The stories you get were from those who really did have something to lose! It's always easier to write about the bad rather than good, is it not? Compare the attraction of Shakespeare's MacBeth with the rather twee rendition of Atticus Finch in Harper Lee's *To Kill a Mockingbird*. A good question for literature students!

Back to the Americans. Took them on a tour of the estate. Let them earmark a nice green site, take their photographs so they got angles and perspective of our castle just right, measure out the land required etc. Took them to dinner in our castle cum hotel, of course—usual crap Chinese banquet type stuff, chickens' feet, sea cucumber, paddy field chicken with chilli and black bean sauce, Mongolian lamb, pigs liver and kidney, turtle soup with floating turtle in it, with loads of bai jiu (Chinese rice wine with a kick like a mule's and an unbelievable afterburn in the throat!) to wash it all down—how is it foreigners always think these are special events? And why is it they think getting trashed on bai jiu should make them special in our eyes? Pathetic really!—and then got down to a contract knowing full well from our point of view you're not allowed to build on designated green sites—China does have an environmental policy in case you hadn't realised so there was never a possibility (certainly not in this case) of getting a licence to build a school on the lush stretch of greenery with its nice view they had chosen. Down payment on the deal—250,000¥ cash up front paid directly to me. Thank you very much! Fapiao? (Receipt to you.) You must be fucking joking? Two copies of the contract : one in English legalese and one in Mandarin in anything but legalese, but both stating that in any dispute it all comes under the laws of China and will be settled in a Chinese court. What fucking joke! Napoleon had the good sense (was it so good?) to set up the Code Napoleon in France but Mao, Mao was so much wiser! Don't write down laws otherwise you will get disputes, you will get precedence etc. Bloody hell, you will have to have lawyers for God's sake! Lawyers! Need I say more? Who was it wrote, "for a Westerner, a contract is a contract, but in China it is a snapshot of a set of arrangements that happened to exist at one time"? Absolutely right! I guess the writer of that must have been screwed several times over with various contracts—stupid bugger!

Well, the Americans waited. And waited. And waited.

Eventually they get in touch. "What's happening?" they ask.

"Waiting to hear from the Government," I reply.

"But we're waiting to hear from you!"

"These things take time," I say. "Patience is a virtue; isn't that what you say?"

"How much time?"

(I think, "Is that a philosophical question or a genuine request for a measurement?")

"I'll try to push them for an answer."

So the Americans waited a bit more. And a bit more. And a bit more.

Eventually I have to give them the bad news.

"Sorry. There's a licence problem. Government isn't giving out any. We can't get the licence for you."

"But Clause 5.1 states . . . ."

"Yes, I am aware of that. Let me clarify the situation. It's not we can't get the licence. I'll rephrase that. I don't know when I can get you the licence. At the moment the government isn't giving out any."

"What are you saying?"

"I don't know when I can get you the licence."

"Meaning?"

Don't these cretins understand English? Maybe not! They are American after all!

"I don't know when I can get you the licence."

I wasn't going to go into the excuse of the green site : why confuse the issue? I don't know if they're still waiting around now for an answer. The silence, as they say, following my news was deafening. I suppose that was their idea of closure! I guess they didn't want to be any more out of pocket than was necessary. Perhaps they went to another site and got ripped off again. I bet they did but they would never admit it. Eventually they will learn.

I never ever tell Mum and Dad about my deals and in this case they were a bit amazed that for about a month and a half I wasn't taking cash out of the family coffers to fund my playboy life style. 250,000¥ cash helped of course but money like that doesn't really go very far, not when you're driving a Ferrari, employing a fatso minder cum driver with a stupid grin and having a different Shelia every night of the week. There's no such thing as a free lunch—even the Yanks would have got that message. All part of the Chinese learning curve!

"Make the lie big, make it simple, keep saying it, and eventually they will believe it." I read that in a history book somewhere.

MICHELLE WONG

D en of Iniquity! That's the name of my new night club in Beijing? Like it? I don't like beating about the bush. My business is in the sex industry. If you like, the customers pay me and my business for the foreplay before the real thing. The three best things in life : a drink before (that's on offer at my clubs) and a cigarette after (if they insist but my clubs are non-smoking havens anyway so that has to be someplace else—and I'm strict about that). Get them in so they can get it on, that's my motto. (That's the second best thing of course for those of you who haven't quite tuned in to my sense of humour yet!) We're open late until early, 7 days a week, 365 days a year (add on the extra day for the leap year).

What's in a name? Quite a lot actually! Well my places speak for themselves (my other club as you know is Sodom and Gommorrah) but what do you make of stupid names like Maya, Club Rouge, Bling, China Doll, The World of Suzie Wong—who the fuck is Suzie Wong?—Christ you have to be getting your pension to know the answer to that!

Want a tour? A real one, not the virtual reality of the web site that is?

Do you like the entrance? Yes, I took that idea from cover of The Rolling Stones' Bigger Bang album—the tongue (red carpet that you walk up) through the mouth under the lips into the Den! Inviting, sexy or what? What does it remind you of? (No need to answer that!) The décor? A combination of Palatinate purple, Russian red and Nazi black with suitable lighting of course—silks and soft furnishings in abundance. That's pretty basic though—what I like are the statues—all illusions to sex naturellement!—got to get the excitement levels stimulated. Over there a life size version of Leda and the Swan. You don't know the myth? Look it up but you can see the swan's got his beak into her so not much imagination or research is needed is it? There's a copy of Michaelangelo's David—not exact because we've added a bit as you can see and it's clearly getting more handling than the gold coloured studs on the doors of The Forbidden City! Over in that corner, Eve biting into her apple (her fruit is getting a fair bit of handling as well from what I can see). There's others. I am sure you can recognise them . . . . Marquis De Sade, Don Juan, Venus De Milo (complete version!), Helen of Troy (It wasn't her face that launched a thousand ships, look at the body, look at the . . . .!), Mao Zedong—sex symbols the lot of them!

Well, maybe Mao was not exactly a sex symbol but he did have plenty of women! (However, it's politically correct to have him there. Gets me brownie points and saves me money!) Sets the right atmosphere, don't you think? Add the music . . . . don't ask me what they play, I just hire the DJ, but it seems to give out the right vibes and it's all part of the sex business all right!

Ah, my clients. They fall into the following categories:-

Chinese men (a) the ones that come to display their wives/girl-friends/concubines on their arms—showy lot that's all. They're the big drinkers—buy bottles of Bollinger, JW Blue Label, Smirnoff, Courvoisier, Grey Goose vodka or whatever. All show—see and be seen! High rollers! (b) the ones who are also big drinkers but not all high rollers and come in the hopeful expectation (more often than not to be disappointed) that they might just click with a Western (or at least Russian/Mongolian) chick. Occasionally one does and when they leave as a couple they can look a bit like Laurel and Hardy—you know who is who! (That's another fine mess they intend to get into!)

Western Women. I feel a bit sad for this lot. They generally come in groups and they can't really expect to pick up a man not with the competition from the Chinese, Mongolian and Russian talent being offered up like a smorgasboord—not even a Chinese one. Some of them are as plump as porpoises and it must be like making love to a bouncy castle when you're in bed with them. (Mind you, some of the Chinese girls are so waif like it must be like making love to a stick insect if you get into bed with them). Often though, they're out on a hen night so they blow a fair bit of cash and get pretty ratted. They can become quite excited and are real ravers when they get carried away even wanting to disrobe themselves occasionally—but we have to be careful of that as there's the plain clothes police around and too much hanky panky can get us closed down . . . . or rather cost me even more backhanders to stay open!

Western men. Need I say more?

Han Chinese, Mongolian and some Russian women. Need I say more?

It all adds up to good business. The object of any business is to make a profit so the cost of drinks is naturally outrageous (55RMB for a very small bottle of Tsingdao!) I leave you to work out the cost of a flute of champagne (and not good champagne at that though the customers are conned into thinking it is!) and we don't do stupid things like happy hour—I'm not running a bloody charity. Food? Of course we do do nibbles—don't laugh, I'm serious! Any bites with lots of salt—makes the clients thirstier and then they'll drink more.

Weekends are packed out—just like what they are, cattle markets—but we do have theme nights on weekdays to draw the crowds in. They are also popular and business is good. Very good! Should I say fucking good? The majority of the clients, I am sure, think so. Themes vary but we have to keep up the right level of titillation (sorry about the pun—no, I'm not really). We have had a Vicars and Tarts night—no problem in getting the latter but we had to do a bit of education to advise our clients about the former! Whacky Teachers and Naughty School Girls night wasn't the best of successes—well, I am sure you know that schools here wear track suits as their uniforms so they didn't quite grasp what we wanted but the teachers seemed well tooled up (sorry about the pun—no, I'm not really) with their canes, belts, plimsolls etc. Mr Men and Little Miss Evening was a hoot though I don't know that Roger Hargreaves or his wife did publish books entitled Mr Prick or Little Miss Nonickers or for that matter, Mr Fuck-Nose/knows! Might have reached and adult audience had they done so! Our Fairy Tale evening had its moments—Rupunzel letting down her hair was a bit too open to wide interpretations as was Jack and the Beanstalk and the Elves and the Shoemaker! Little Red Riding Hood picked up a lot of wolves though and Little Miss Muffet managed to get more than her fair share of spiders. Yes, we had the Little Jack Horners—see 1 (b) above under

Clients! We did have a "come as your favourite character" from book, stage or screen night. Wow, that proved pretty sensational! The woman who came as Eve—just top to toe see-through body stocking certainly got a lot of attention and didn't need to eat an apple (or buy a drink all evening come to that!) and the fellah that came as Richard Branson had the girls (I can't say virgins because that would be a gross exaggeration) clinging to him all night . . . . and following him when he left. Come to think of it, he was such a dead ringer for Richard Branson I think it really was him. Must have been—he's not a character from book, stage or screen is he? Oh, he wrote an autobiography? They all do that so it doesn't count! Guess he was in the capital for the night and just was taking some time out! It's amazing what happens in this city! Did you ask about Beach parties? Oh, they're so passé, don't you think?

We've only been open just over two months and, believe it or not, I've almost clawed back my investment already. Good business, eh? Good sex business! I love it! Not sure where I go from here. I've two thriving (and heaving) clubs in different parts of the city and don't want to get into a situation of expansion and the law of diminishing returns. There's a growing gay and lesbian scene in China of course but I don't want to go down that path yet. Bit too dodgy! But it will happen eventually. I am sure of that. The way China is going, it's inevitable!

FU

Yes, poor Eleanor is currently banged up for her silly little drug habit but let's not dwell on that, not for now anyway. Where was I? Ah yes.

So there's Annie and me on the Metro on Friday looking shagged out (not literally—well at least not then!) and Eleanor looking a fresh as a daisy and bloody smartly dressed : dress by Chloe, shoes by Tod's, hair by Vidal Sassoon, accessories by Gucci and they were the real thing, not your Yan Xiang market fakes. Smiles at first then chat . . . . Where are you from? Where do you work? What do you do? How long have you been living in Shanghai? Where do you live? How often do you get back home? Are you happy? You know the kind of thing. Annie and I splurted it all out . . . . Changzhou, China Telecom, Happiness? What's that? We don't do happiness! We phone the Samaritans . . . . the lot. Eleanor though was a little more vague, definitely more reticent on her answers to these questions—strange since in appearance at least she gave the impression of being a very confident young (or was she really that young?) lady. Then, almost out of the blue and almost as an aside or non-sequitor, she asked, "What do you guys do on weekends?"

"As little as possible," I said wearily.

"Recover, of course!" joked Annie.

Both replies were right of course. Basically all we ever did was sleep and then, when we got up, we would cook some food and watch DVDs, one of the few "luxuries" we could afford—all copies of course, 5RMB a go here and all the latest releases. Intellectual property rights? Don't do intellectual property rights! (Watching DVDs was one of the ways I learned my American and English vernacular . . . . but not the only one!)

"Never go out?" she asked.

"Can't afford to," we chorused.

"Well, ladies," she smiled, this has to be your lucky day! C'mon. My treat this weekend. Tomorrow night, right? Long Bar—part of the Portman Ritz Carlton, Shanghai Centre in Nanjing Xi Road. Meet me there. I'll shout you a meal and some drinks—late on mind. Say 9.30. 10.00? You can find it, can't you? All the taxi drivers know it."

"Taxis!" we exclaimed.

"O.K.," she said. "Metro Line 2. Nanjing Xi Road, Exit 4 and walk up the road and it's on the right or Jing'an Si, Exit 4 and walk down the road and it's on the left. Oh, and by the way, make yourselves look lovely!"

And so she took her farewell.

Annie and I looked at each other. A free meal and drinks! Sounded too good to miss out on. Bit late in the day though ....

JENNY JING

It's a real privilege to me to be able to contribute to this small volume of prose that will give you an insight into China today.

I'm a Beijinger and proud of it. Lived and worked her all my life (apart from a couple of years spent studying in the UK) and seen and experienced at first hand many of the great changes that have happened to our great nation all have which have been reflected in this, our capital city, over the past years. Beijing gives you a great sense of history and even when I drive round the city today in my silver Audi A3 convertible I feel it, even though most of the city as it was has disappeared under the relentless bulldozers of the property developers and been replaced by architectural carbuncles of steel and reflecting glass curtains towering into the haze of the polluted sky.

Mind you, in that respect, the city and its development reflects our lives. I remember wearing the drab, ill-fitting, coarse, green uniforms of the red guard, eating from a common, enamel rice bowl and frantically waving my little red book in my middle school in the late sixties but now I've got all make over creams, lipsticks, fragrances and white facials from Dior and Chanel, wear the best fashions of the top designer brands (the real McCoy—that's not a brand name by the way) and I eat out at Haiku, The Orchard, Brasserie Flo, Alemeda, Let's Burger and the like. I suppose, as Luke, my Australian friend and colleague, comments, "The city, its buildings and its people—all just a makeover of lipstick and rouge!"

I've often wondered, by the way, about the little red book and thought it really should be called the little read book. All it was useful for was waving around (thankfully being pocket size, with a plastic cover and printed on thin, crap paper it was quite light and portable) as a talisman to bring out the great and the good (?) to parade benignly before us, the heaving mass of semi-literate, youthful humanity who didn't know any better but were bloody glad to get time out of school! And in some cases, comrades came from all over China so they got free travel and a bit of a holiday in our great capital city. Lucky blighters! Perhaps we all ought to be thankful very few people did read it and probably those who did hadn't a clue what is was all about anyway.

Yes I was a fledgling red guard but not one of those aggressive ones who went around making people eat shit, having struggle sessions, smashing up houses, destroying the olds and generally embarking on a careers of mayhem and destruction—come to think of it not unlike what our modern government is and has been doing in all our major cities of late! Oh, and I think some of those sort of things feature as behaviour in Europe nowadays? And yes, we got those directives about eschewing the four olds . . . . etc The Chinese have a passion for numbers—the Four Olds, the Four Modernisations, The Hundred Flowers movement, PLA's Three Main Rules of Discipline and Eight Points for Attention etc . . . Yes, indeed, we Chinese love numbers—part of our psyches! And we're good at arithmetic—read *Outliers* by what's his name to find out why! Eight is lucky, four most certainly isn't—in some office and apartment blocks have you noticed there's no fourth floor? Do you think there's a gap and floors 5 and above float on thin air above floor 3? As a realty agent I know there's a kind of gap—there is between all floors!—perhaps I shouldn't say that! Sichuan province and its inhabitants know that, to their cost!

After the heady days and shenanigans of the sixties I settled back into studies, got a good degree from Beida and went to work in real estate. There was plenty to do as the city was in expansion mode (when isn't it, you may well ask?)—we were moving out and beyond the third ring road then, now we have six ring roads—it's as if we are trying to emulate Saturn! Well Dubai wishes

Though actually I sometimes wonder because they seem so naïve that maybe they do need such educational institutions!), recreation facilities etc. It's here the entrepreneurial spirit of the locals—yes by that I mean all of us clever Chinese—comes in. Let's keep things simple. Here we are in the great, 1.3 billion food chain of Chinese land owners—What a fucking joke! In Communist China where everything, including the money (Renmimbi) and a square in every city (Renmin guangchang) belongs to the people i.e. The great proletarian, the great totalitarian state?—surveyors, property developers, realty companies, construction companies, material and equipment suppliers, drivers, itinerant workers, each and everyone wants, indeed needs a piece of the action. We all want, indeed need a share of all this but it's never share and share alike. We are not that egalitarian! Each individual negotiates his/her added percentage against the percentage of the main person he/she is dealing with. We have our salaries, we have our bonuses, we have our annual hong bao at the Spring Festival and we have our cut (untaxed of course and handed over in dirty RMB notes!) from any deal which we make. Not the black, but the yellow market economy. Communism with a Chinese twist/spin? Fortunately, Johnny Foreigner has not caught on to this aspect of our society and rarely, if ever, questions the highly inflated prices he has to pay for such services in the property market. Strange, since I think, no, indeed I know, things are not dissimilar in the UK for example (and I am sure in most of Europe and the USA). It takes one to know one I guess and from their supposedly Christian point of view, "Let he who is without sin, cast the first stone." How I love those moral imperatives.

This scenario has not diminished over the years (thankfully it's flourished and continues to do so) since Deng Xiaoping told us we didn't need to be poor to be a communist and was subsequently credited with opening up China. "It doesn't matter if a cat is black or white as long as it catches mice," the great man said (in Chinese of course). Obviously he most certainly did not read the little red/read book! Even Chairman Mao realised this and that's why he was purged twice—what a survivor though!

Anyway, I, and many like me, are among the immediate beneficiaries. You can gather from what I have said earlier on, my life style is good and I actually own, yes own, a villa (fully renovated to British kite mark standards I might add) where I live in legend Garden and I own, yes own, an apartment there as well (also fully renovated to British kite mark standards I might add) which I rent out privately—am not sure I should have written that and must only hope someone in the tax authorities is not reading this or I might find my private RMB stash being somewhat depleted. Just to clarify things, I won't get done for tax fraud and imprisoned or have to pay back taxes or anything as stupid as that, but I will have to pay someone in the tax bureau off with regard to this 'hidden income.' In the great 1.3 billion food chain of Chinese national government officials, local government officials, national administrators, local administrators, national tax bureau employees, local tax bureau employees, national tax collectors, local tax collectors . . . . etc . . . . I am sure you get the picture!

Oh, dear, I've just noticed the time . . . . just gone 2.00 on Friday afternoon. A small matter of a weekly routine. Excuse me but I must rush. Got to pick my lovely 13 year old daughter up from her weekly boarding school. It's about 45 minutes drive out from my office on the outskirts of the city . . . . beyond the sixth ring road . . . .

BILL

I'm now in the shoe business out here. A bit of a jump from education (but we all have to get out of that profession if we want to stay sane, don't we?) to making shoes but in a former life (that is another story) i.e. when I was younger, I did work for that rather prestigious of shoe companies in the UK, Clarks—who now manufacture their iconic desert boot in 'Nam! So that came in handy when I applied for the job as well as the fact that the owner of the company was a neighbour in my apartment block whom I'd got to know having the odd beer or two down the Full House One Bar. Then of course there's my degree and my specialism in materials testing. All part of a winning CV. Got a factory in the Jiuting area of Shanghai. It's a bit far from my new apartment in the city but not too difficult to get to provided you choose the right times of the day .... otherwise you'll spend more time in traffic than actually at work. A definite feature of modern China. I'm the Managing Director of a company that's actually owned by a Tiawanese businessman—there's a lot of

Taiwanese owned businesses in China—don't believe all you read in the paper about the "stand offs" between the mainland and Taiwan. I'm the only white man in the set up but fortunately the supervisory and managerial staff speak English even though the work force, of course, is entirely local. My own job and having been in this country for quite a time has given me an interesting insight into the work ethic of the Chinese. Let me give you a picture of it.

Despite all their best efforts, the Christian missionaries who infiltrated China in the 19th century failed to imbue their would-be converts with the Protestant work ethic. Fortunately also, in the twentieth century, the corporate work strategy of their neighbours, the Japanese, is also as alien to the Chinese as are the Japanese themselves. This means the words, "work, rest and play" are not as differentiated in the Chinese psyche as they are in other cultures. As a result, they do not consider their days necessarily structured into such compartments but are more conscious of the sum of these parts rather than the individual parts themselves. (Quite a philosophical, sociological, psychological introduction there when you think about it : and there's more to come!)

Now the Chinese have a reputation for hard work. This has largely come about because there is still a lot of physically demanding work done by Chinese workers and because there is still a lot of drudgery in the work.

(Tourists love to see the industrious peasant toiling in the paddy fields, the cyclist straining to carry his whole family, house and possessions on his bike etc.) However, on close inspection, individuals take ages over doing whatever they have to to occupy their time. Parkinson's Law—check it out on Google. For example, it takes three people a whole morning in China to cut a moderate size lawn. There is the worker with the motor mower (yes, motor mower!) who mows up and down the grass. When the tray is full of grass (about every three or four lengths) along comes the collector of the grass with a black, polythene bag and takes off the tray and dumps the grass into the bag and replaces the tray. The bag of grass is then taken to a cyclist with a large pannier or maybe even a small trailer space on the back of his bike who has been waiting patiently at the side of the lawn and the bag with the grass is deposited in the pannier or trailer. He then cycles off to the nearby dump to empty the grass out of the bag and bring it back to the collector of the grass. The worker with the motor mower (yes motor mower!) then mows up and down the grass. When the tray is full . . . . and the cycle continues as its leisurely pace. Each part looks physically hard and, to a certain extent is, but why should one man do the whole job when three can be gainfully employed in doing it?

(Get things in perspective. This country has 1.3 billion population. If one man was allowed to do the work of three, which may be logically and ergonomically possible, what would the unemployment rate be like? Two-thirds of the work force on the dole? Could you live with that? What was your name again? Margaret Thatcher? Forgotten who she was already?)

No. In reality, the Chinese are—how shall we say?—lazy, and that I honestly mean as a compliment, not a criticism. C'mon! We'd all like to work but to be able to take out time over what we do. If, as in the case of China, the population allows it, then the myriad of workers who make up the work force know there's plenty around to do the jobs so they have, in the words of Louis Armstrong's hit, "All the time in the world . . . ." And good luck to them. So you still think laziness is a bad thing : then why do you do the lottery every week? Are you going to give all those millions away when you win and keep on working? Truth to tell, we envy the Chinese and this in-built laziness of theirs : we want it for ourselves but all we ever get is a guilt trip if we take time out when we should be working. Ah, the protestant work ethic . . . . where would we be without it?

The real beauty of the system here though is the way each job, each task builds in the work, rest and play elements. Returning to the grass cutting scenario, whilst the grass is being dumped, the mower operator will casually pass the time of day possibly having a fag and chatting to the black bag carrier. He will definitely not go on working because that would set up a production line of sorts and would smack of efficiency—far too Germanic! Worse still, too Japanese! When the grass has been dumped, the black bag carrier will go and casually pass the time of day possibly having (another) fag and chatting with the cyclist. The blend of productive activity, smoking, chatting is the perfect way of working. Work, rest and play (chatting/fag smoking!) This is to be seen wherever you go.

In the department stores, notice the assistants. You cannot not notice them as they are the liveried people (nearly always female) standing around the counters. You may think some of the uniforms are ostentasiously gaudy, inappropriate, unsuited to the wearers, unfashionable even, and you would be right. However it helps identify who's who in the store. (Having said that, have you ever eaten in T G I Fridays and seen what they wear there? Short black skirts held up by stars and stripes bracers, Doc Martin boots, no socks, headbands, various badges and necklaces, hair plaited and tied in pigtails—and that's just the fellahs! Are they all auditioning for a part in *Joseph and His Amazing Technicolour Dreamcoat?*) Anyway, the assistants are there to sell you the merchandise. Now buy something. You like the set of cloissonee chopsticks—just right for that mad Aunt of yours who advised you not to go to China because there's no milk available there, if they are not abandoning babies they are eating them and it's a communist country . . . . it's red! You pick the chopsticks up, get out the money and . . . . the assistant waves a finger and gets out a little wad of paper. You think you're going to be done for shoplifting or trying to bribe an assistant (no, that's ridiculous—bribing's not an offence in P R China), consider a life sentence in the rat-infested cells of the nearest prison, having a diet of rice and water and worse still, wearing an ill fitting Chairman Mao suit with arrows on it is not on and are about to make a run for it . . . . but no! The assistant motions you to return the chopsticks and starts writing on the wad of paper which you now see to be self-duplicating receipts. You watch and wait. After about 2 minutes she tears off a wad of paper and hands it to you. The top copy is white and there's yellow and blue and pink and possibly other coloured copies beneath. You look nonplussed. You want the chopsticks, not paper with Chinese writing on. She points to another counter and indicates you must take the wad of paper there. With trepidation you head off to this counter—for all you know you could be bearing your own death sentence like Rosencrantz and Guildenstern but, when you get to this counter, there's another liveried assistant who takes the wad of paper from you. While you watch she separates out the bits of paper, gets a stamp, hits it in the red ink pad and bangs it on to the various bits of paper and maybe even adds a bit of writing to them herself. Then she tells you the price in Chinese which you don't understand so she gets out a calculator and bashes the charge into the little screen, holds it up so you can see how much you owe. She then takes money from you, counts it, checks it and shoves it in a drawer. Keeping the white top copy from the wad of paper, she returns the rest to you and points you back in the direction in which you came and stuffs the white retained copy into another drawer usually filled to the brim with crumpled white to copies. This has taken about four of five minutes or possibly longer and has allowed the first assistant to have a breather probably during which time she may chat to her mates or even fall asleep (see later), and by the time you return she takes the bits of paper back off you, separates them out, smiles and hands you one of the coloured, self-duplicated copies of the paper and a green box.

The green box contains the chopsticks, you discover. Here two people are doing the job of one, not quite as good as the grass cutting group but assistants work indoors, are provided with a ostentasiously gaudy, inappropriate, unsuitable, unfashionable uniform and probably get about 10RMB more in the salaries each week. Now try buying four or more different items from four different stalls, taking your paper collection to the cashier and paying for them in one go. Then see if you remember the right stall to take the right bits of paper back to. It becomes like that card game where the cards are face down and you've got match pairs—a real test of memory and not without its skill element as well. It's great being a customer in a department store. Much more fun than Marks and Spencer on Oxford Street or in Nanjing Xi Lu—yes the famous store has now hit Shanghai!

As you look around you see many more desirable jobs combining exactly the right amount of physical or mental action together with time to rest and play. In the U K Lollipop Ladies/Men who do the wonderful job of seeing children safely across the street are invariably retired individuals wanting a couple of hours 'en plein air' daily. They also like being abused by the little and not so little ones they shepherd across the road : it reminds them of their youth, keeps them 'in touch' makes them feel young again. Here such persons are employed not for children but for the whole population. Making sure the crowds get across the streets in city centres is a real vocation—and, in The Chinese Way, a part vacation as well. It's very stressful—crowd control's not easy, there's always a few people intent on suicide while the traffic is in full swing and therefore, the sharp blasts on the whistles, the frantic waving of the red flag—it just has to be red, doesn't it, but it doesn't have the gold stars on—and the string of verbal abuse needs to be well timed and well aimed. But there's a chance to meet ordinary people, have a quick chat to the cyclists, pedestrians, bus drivers, lorry drivers (the traffic's often grid-locked, by the way—well, it has to be occasionally, how else would the job of driving anything contain the three elements of work, rest and play?) have a fag, chat to your opposite number across the road etc while the traffic lights are against you and so on. Oh, yes, didn't I mention they do have traffic lights and there is the green man flashing (tired English joke) but did you really think the traffic would be so obedient of lights? And anyway, the road traffic act here allows for traffic and pedestrians to move at the same time—well, it adds to the fun; isn't it just boring to cross the street safely on a pedestrian crossing with all the traffic stopped for you, humble pedestrian? Traffic lights?—No, it has to be people to get things done. Again, these traffic officers are liveried persons .... but it's best not to speak ill of government supplied uniforms .... but they are brown! Well, it's a bit of a dangerous job!

And, writing of traffic, we naturally can consider the driver's job. Many middle and senior managers in companies like me have drivers. Why? Well, have you tried crossing a road in China? (See the above paragraph.) I rest my case. But if you really want to hike your personal insurance up by 100% and reduce your life expectancy by double figures, by all means, drive yourself. Cycle, even, if life's really that bad and your wife really doesn't understand if they turn up somewhere on or around 09.00 or 10.00 that's usually good enough. After all, it saves lame excuses like the chain fell off my bike, the bus was too crowded I had to walk, it was raining heavily and the streets were flooded, I had to go back because I forgot to bring my packed lunch (what's that?) and obviates the necessity of phoning in to say, "I'm sorry, I am going to get into work a little late today." Bring a book to read so as not to suffer from too much eye-screen problems from word processing or accessing e-mails, and you can always play card games on the computer in the hours between those serious seconds of concentrated activity. You may even fall asleep slumped across your desk when the stress is too much. Such scenes of high powered inertia abound in office life.

Sleep. (Macbeth could never have been Chinese because, according to Shakespeare he murdered sleep, whereas Samuel Taylor Coleridge apostrophised it in *The Ancient Mariner*—that's what opium does for you—so he must be well-revered out here!) Rest! They have the ability of cats to sleep any time, any place, anywhere. The driver moves over to sleep in the passenger seat of his idle car having dropped you off and now waiting for his next big task of taking you home. If it's a hot day, he opens the doors of the car to have air conditioning. (Well, he may well have removed his shoes . . . .!) The builders sleep on the matting stretched across the bamboo scaffolding. The cyclist sleeps you are not properly qualified and can be certain to make a hash of the translation from Chinese into English.

Vetinary Surgeon. Not much demand though you might get a job in the hospitals if you're not careful . . . . or maybe on those wonderful, outdoor markets or even in a restaurant. You can't expect the exorbitant pay levels doing this though that you would get in The West.

Dietician. Have you seen what they eat out here? Worse still, do you *know* what they eat out here. I hope you've read what I wrote before and this statement is therefore redundant.

Work study engineer. (Also referred to as a Time and Motion Man—a great misnomer, don't you think?) Who needs them when you have all the (wo)manpower you need? Robotic and Automated machinery manufacturer. Who needs them when you have all the (wo)manpower you need?

Town and Country Planner. Far too big a task even for a country of 1.3 billion people. And are you really telling me there's any urban planning in this country? Have a look around the Jing An temple area of Nanjing Xi Road—Wheelock tower, Puli hotel, Swissotel, City Shopping Mall and there's the Jing An Buddhist temple crouching in the shadows of all these places. Now a new Kerry Centre and Shangri-La hotel is being added. Did anyone realise it was there when planning the building of these giant monstrosities around it? Planning? It revolves around kick-backs obviously!

Chopsticks or disposable, slip-on mules manufacturer. Too much like hard work! You might actually have to set up a production line. Far too Germanic. Worse still, too Japanese.

Environmental Health Officer. Not to be confused with Health and Safety at Work Officer but not an attractive job for not dissimilar reasons. Those open-fronted, little cafes and restaurants are really inviting, don't you think? Do you think this is the country where the expression about "the pot calling the kettle" black comes from or "out of the frying pan, into the fire" as well?

Self-adhesive postage stamp manufacturer. Who needs them when there's plenty of messy glue available?

Anything to do with karaoke or line dancing.

All in all ergonomics in China is an exciting, enthralling area of study. Certainly worthy of a PhD thesis! Who was it wrote, "I like work. I could sit and watch it for hours." Was that in Mao's Little Red Book? Whatever, must have been written by a Chinese!

One little addition about pay but I really don't know if this applies throughout the working, resting and playing world of China. We have a massive work force at our factory—nearly 5,000 operatives in total! We decided we wanted to put them on the BACS scheme so they could get their money paid directly into their bank accounts. We choose the China Construction Bank—the most aptly named bank in China—their premises are always being rebuilt, renovated or whatever. Anyway, they were very wary of this but we explained to them how it worked and gave them their bank cards for the hole in the wall and even showed them how to use it. Come the first pay day, the bank credited the accounts and we issued pay slips (and showed their tax and welfare payments) to one and all. At the end of each shift (we have to work 3* x 8 hr shifts a day—you will understand if you have read what I have written previously!) we were surprised to see all the operatives queuing at the three ATMs we had on site. Each and everyone drew out his/her salary there and then. Not sure what the bank thought—certainly didn't make any money in interest as the money couldn't have been in the accounts for more than a few hours. We should have stuck to pay packets! Crazy!

(* Three shifts—two for the real brands and overnight shift for the fakes—can you tell the difference—between the fakes and the real brands that is?)

WU DABIN &
JIANG SHULIN

You may think working at an international school as a maintenance guy is dull and boring. Not so! The one I work at is crazy and, from what I've learned from mates elsewhere in Shanghai, the others are not much better. Thankfully I and my team are fully qualified and trained electricians, plumbers, builders, surveyors, gas-fitters, painters and decorators, IT and telephone engineers, qualified drivers (HGV and PSV), carpenters, cabinet makers, metalworkers, car mechanics, swimming pool maintenance managers, masseurs etc so we can right the wrongs that occur on the premises and boy, are there plenty of wrongs! And maybe soon we will qualify as EFL teachers!

To begin at the beginning, as they say. We opened only 5 years ago. The opening? What a fucking joke!

Mr Harding and his staff—he's a great guy by the way—more of him later!—had prepared everything to greet the newly arriving hordes of kids. They were all prepared. But they weren't prepared for the way they were about to be dropped in it by their devious Chinese owner.

Well, the buses rolled in, the kids got off, were greeted and chaperoned to their classrooms and all seemed well. It was, by the way, a blazingly hot and humid day just as we usually get at the end of August/start of September in Shanghai. The forecast for the days ahead suggested this spell of weather i.e. blazingly hot and humid, would be prolonged as indeed we usually get this at the end of August/start of September in Shanghai! Harding, looking pleased with himself, smartly turned out in pin-striped suit, college tie and all that—impressive!—stood on the steps of the main entrance perfectly satisfied that all was underway with the type of precision that he was to become admired for. Mr Xie, the Chinese owner, was beside him also looking pleased but about to give his appointee the bad news.

"Excellent start," he said. "Excellent." Then he added, sotto voce, "Oh by the way, there's no air conditioning in the cafeteria and gymnasium! Oh, and there's no hot water for showers in the gym either."

Harding's face turned purple : something it had a habit of doing throughout his incumbency of his office over the next four years thanks to the deceitful and devious machinations of the Machievellian Mr Xie. It would be impossible for children to sit and eat in a non air-conditioned cafeteria and being involved in sports in the gym without even recourse to decent showers . . . . and he was responsible for these children and to their parents. So, for the first six weeks or so the auditorium saw productions of the banquet scene from MacBeth while the gym entertained the various physical gymnastic manoeuvres of Tom Stoppard's Jumpers!

On reflection when Harding's face turned purple, and, as I said it had a habit of doing so throughout his incumbency, he always seemed to solve his problems. Not sure it did him much good, though. A variation on your Incredible Hulk character I guess?

There was more to follow. We have a swimming pool. That should have opened 5 years ago when the school did as well, but it didn't. Thanks to building and licence delays (standard problems in China but even these Chinese owners seemed to have ways of making such problems worse!) it opened 4 years ago and the pools (it has a senior one and a junior one, 25 metres each in length) were built back to front i.e. when the kids came out of the changing room they were faced with the deep end rather than the shallow end. Some judicious, protective fencing had to be quickly installed, thanks to your truly! Then the walls did not account for the condensation from the heating in the pool so the tiles were constantly streaming with water not unlike the sides of the Portman Ritz-Carlton building in the Shanghai Centre (but that there is a design feature, ours was not exactly intended to be a design feature!) and the ceiling paint was also not of the right type so big black flakes of paint were peeling off and landing in the pool making it seem like a new breed of flying (but actually these floated rather than flew) fish had emerged in Shanghai. Harding with his purple features had to close the pool for over 6 weeks not long after its official opening because of these problems!

The laboratories are worthy of a visit. The visitor will see nicely sized work places, plenty of space between the benches and good prep rooms but are the students all seriously over-height challenged? The benches seem so low? Ah, no! The rooms were fully completed before gas was fitted. When the gas pipes were fitted they stood proud of the then flooring. You can't lower floor but you can raise them and so another floor level had to be put on to cover the pipes otherwise they would have been a severe health and safety hazard. A kind of Brobdingnagian affair I guess. And there's certainly still a safety hazard given that the smoke alarms are switched off in all the labs (and where would be the most likely place for a fire to start in a school?) because whenever the gas is switched on for the Bunsen burners the fire alarms sound and it's 'everybody out!' (The test tubes, supplied by honourable Chinese companies, also seem to have a habit of melting as well!)

blowing all the fuses. Lack of sealants round door frames and between walls and floors which means armies of ants parade up the walls and along corridors during hot, humid weather (such as we often get in Shanghai). Railings and fences that start off painted in a shiny, deep blue (one of the school colours) but rapidly, like chameleons, turn to a rust brown in keeping with the outside window frames of the school and all the apartment blocks surrounding the school premises. An all weather playing surface the surface of which is hardly all weather—well we often get plenty of wet weather and hot weather in Shanghai and regrettably it cannot accommodate both . . . . but then again it cannot accommodate just one type of weather! I could go on . . . .

You will see now that it is fortunate that I and my team are fully qualified and trained electricians, plumbers, builders, surveyors, gas-fitters, painters and decorators, IT and telephone engineers, qualified drivers (HGV and PSV), carpenters, cabinet makers, metalworkers, car mechanics, swimming pool maintenance managers, masseurs etc. And you thought we were bullshitting about all those qualifications! Never a dull moment for us . . . .

That's my husband! Having a good moan but always smiling about things! He really does work very hard but he's very clever in his work . . . . and I don't mean because he's a fully qualified and trained . . . . you know it all by now! No, he's a good manager of his work force and he order about to do as many menial tasks as they wish. If only they knew what he really thought of them! A kind of throwback to the era of "No dogs, no Chinese" (check your history of Shanghai if that reference is lost on you) and the opium addicted society foisted on us by fat British guanxi bastards (easily recognisable because they're white and fat!) But this pays dividends. Apart from receiving his lousy stipend from the tight-arsed school owners, he is often showered with cash in hand bonuses from the parents association, individual teaching staff and some individual parents and given presents such as bottles of scotch, bottles of wine, boxes of chocolates, baskets of fruit and vegetables, clothes (well hand me downs—those are a bit insulting, don't you think—we're not beggars, after all?), and meals out at nice restaurants (when I am often invited to join him). On top of this he is also occasionally asked to do some work off site at the apartments or homes of ex-pat staff and/or parents mainly because they cannot get off their lazy backsides to do such simple things as mend handles on cupboard doors, construct a simple barbecue set from Carrefour (even though they have got all the diagrams in pictures in the box with the contents!), fix dripping taps, fix a dripping shower, fix their water boiler, fix their toilet flushing system, mend a broken bed-side lamp, rewire an electrical plug, wash their cars, put up a shelf, assemble an Ikea bookshelf (even though they have got all the diagrams in pictures in the box with the contents!), mend their child's bicycle, re-align their (illegal!) satellite dish or whatever. What a fucking joke! But an expensive one for the ex-pats of course as this kind of labour is definitely not cheap in China! I sometimes say to him he should advertise in Yellow Pages—oh, yes, we have English editions in Shanghai . . . . especially for ex-pats who cannot get off their lazy backsides but want their fingers to do the walking—isn't that what the advert said?

You know it really is lucky that he's a fully qualified and trained electrician, plumber, builder, surveyor, gas-fitter, painter and decorator, IT and telephone engineer, qualified driver (HGV and PSV), carpenter, cabinet maker, metalworker, car mechanic, swimming pool maintenance manager . . . . and for me anyway, a masseur! My husband, Wu Dabin. Don't you just love him? I do!

MICHELLE WONG

I believe they have told you I am Hong Kongese. Mustn't say this too loudly but I am not really. I was born in Shanghai in 1967 and Mum and Dad (bright parents that they are!) made a sharp exit from mainland China with me wrapped in swaddling clothes so that they could avoid the coming catastrophe of the Cultural Revolution. They were also ingenious enough to wrap a whole lot of cash in my swaddling clothes so that on arrival in the island city they weren't like the more dense of their erstwhile comrades i.e. destitute. What insight and foresight they had! They used their money wisely : first to get me registered as born in Hong Kong so I have a Hong Kong and British passport and second to set up a restaurant (outdoors that is!) in Temple Street. As Hong Kong grew, so did their business and so they could afford a superior, British education for me. I am truly blessed with my parents and they now still live in Hong Kong (no money under the floorboards to lure them back to the mainland—they wisely took it all with them) and I visit them as often as I can. I married a Hong

Kong fashion designer (he now still lives in Hong Kong and I visit him as often as I can) and we have a wonderful daughter, Elisabeth, who lives with me and who attends Lancing College international school here in Beijing so she, too, is getting a superior British education. Many of my and her Chinese friends envy that but they should get themselves a foreign passport and then they could send their offspring to the international schools that are now a feature of our major cities here in China. Anyway, why did I come back to the land of my birth, you may well ask?

Well, just as the Cultural Revolution created about a 10-12 year cultural desert in the mainland so the opening up in the later 70s/early 80s really did open up opportunities galore. We had made money in Hong Kong and my parents always lavished me with plenty of it so why not put it to good use? I also spoke Cantonese, English (thanks to my superior British education) and Mandarin, thanks to my parents who found it difficult even to learn Cantonese so always spoke to me in Chinese! And, by the way, they still struggle with learning the Hong Kong language despite their being domiciled in the island city. I also knew about the restaurant business, again thanks to my parents, and knowing the Chinese penchant for food—if it's got two or more legs and moves, eat it!—I guessed this was the best way to get started. Why choose Beijing? Capital city, of course and, just as my parents got

One evening into my restaurant came a big boss and his family. How did I know? Well, he was dressed appallingly and looked more like a slops man* than a senior manager but his wife was dripping in designer wear (the real thing!) with appropriate accessories but had trouble in walking steadily in shoes with 5 inch stiletto heels. His teenage son was also dripping in designer wear and he had difficulty in walking steadily in the latest, multicoloured, all singing and dancing and light flashing 4 inch soled Nike trainers, and he looked and acted like a real spoilt brat. They arrived in a top of the range model, silver Mercedes and his driver was a young looking fatso with a huge grin on his face. That grin was permanently attached it seemed. The boss invited his driver to join them. They ordered practically the whole menu and the family ate hardly anything : spoilt brat managed to complain about everything and kept saying he wished they'd gone to Pizza Hut as he really was starving but this food was unpalatable (not the word he used as he didn't have a vocabulary of words of more than two syllables) but Fatso managed to gobble his way through a pretty gargantuan amount and was given the nod to have what remained as a take away. I personally thanked slops man and his family for favouring me with their custom and gave him my business card and he kindly gave his to me. Useful. The Chinese handshake!

(*Slops man is one of the Chinese 'untouchables' and a nocturnal creature. He comes out the end of each day's dealings in restaurants cycling along on his bike with two huge, plastic blue (well they should be that colour but are somewhat stained by use!) pannier tubs at the bag into which is loaded to overflowing all the day's detritus, kitchen left overs and restaurant's uneaten food and undowned drink. Once loaded to overflowing he cycles off into the darkness and is not seen until the next night and each night thereafter. He leads a seriously sad, solitary existence. No one would want to get near him or his bike—smelt smells are grim but those unsmelt are grimmer! Enough said!)

But back to my visitor. His name was Zhang Xiaobo. He was a government official, a high ranking one and clearly had responsibility for setting up government deals abroad. He was, so I learned, shit rich and was busily engaged in building an exact replica of Neuschwanstein Castle in Germany on the outskirts of Beijing. Shit rich and a mad bastard with it! It takes all sorts. This 'folly' was nearing completion and I drove out to see it. There it was in the middle of the green belt (as it then was) of Beijing. I did a double-take . . . . Am I in China? Am I in Germany? Where the fuck am I? Confused and confusing. Fucking stupid, these Chinese! However, it offered me an opportunity. I learned that this monstrosity of a building was going in part to be used as a hotel so I contacted

Zhang Xiaobo (he used the English name David with foreigners and he considered me one in a kind of way with my HK background) and asked if he was interested in my doing the catering. He wasn't : not because he didn't like the fare we offered but it was "too Chinese/too Cantonese and would not appeal to the wider international clientele" whom he thought would definitely be attracted to the hotel. What a fucking joke! It's so remote, hideous and ridiculous it only ever gets used for those who don't know any better i.e. the non-discerning cadre members'meetings and those who still believe in weddings. Have you checked out its occupancy rate? Anyway he did give me a contract for part catering for the soft opening which was going to be held a few months down the road when everything was complete. Well, it was a start and I did an impressive job, though I say it myself, and apart from winning his favour I managed to meet and butter up/curry favour with (well, I was doing the catering!) several Beijing officials at this soft opening. Subsequent freebie dinners for them, their friends and relatives at Kuaizi paid off and I obtained my licence to open Sodom & Gomorrah in Houhai. Not the best of locations but a start. With various theme nights such as Pee in your Pants night (I did write "pee" not "cream"), Babes in the Woods Night, Miss Wet 'T Shirt night (yes, a bit clichéd but China had only recently come out of the dark ages of The Cultural Revolution), Ticket to

Ride(no, we weren't issuing the tickets : that was down to individuals!) Night (with a great live Beatles Tribute Band from Japan), Oh what a lovely .... (fill in the blank) Night, Beijing Broads, Mongolian Molls and Shanghai Slags Night and pole dancers every night of the week (and I even got the Japanese World Champions over after a couple of years—boy were we packed to the rafters then .... standing room only—(pun absolutely intended) we gained a great reputation and started to pull in the punters big time. Subsequent freebie evenings for the Beijing officials, their male friends and relatives at Sodom and Gomorrah and I obtained my second licence to open Den of Iniquity! A much better location for this club in the heart of Gonti Bei Lu and with a reputation well established along the road in Houhai ("Den of Iniquity brought to you by the same company that brought you Sodom and Gomorrah!") we have never looked back. Check my ratings in The Beijinger, That's Beijing and all the local weekly, bi-weekly and monthly magazines if you don't believe me. Better still, come and see for yourselves—but don't forget the readies and/or the plastic—I'm not running a charity.

Interestingly enough, that real spoilt brat who came with his Mum and Dad to my restaurant all those years ago is now a real spoilt, grown up brat. He now frequents Den of Iniquity—it's nearer his home than Sodom & Gomorrah. Still always dripping in designer wear and he has difficulty in walking in his always brand new crocodile, alligator, snake, mole, kangaroo, koala, duck-bill platypus or whatever skin (sometimes a combination of all of those I think) shoes. He also still thinks the open neck, multi-coloured, gaudy silk shirt with hairy (fake in his case) chest and gold (not fake in his case) medallion, Gucci (not fake in his case) shades and grey, slim-line farrahs with a crease sharp enough to shave a mouse, to be butch, but all that's rather more bitch than butch nowadays, isn't it? What a sight he is! He is driven to and from the venue usually in his top of the range model black Mercedes by his driver, an older looking (but instantly recognisable) fatso with a huge grin on his face. That grin is still permanently attached. Occasionally, Peter, as he likes to call himself (real name Zhang Xie) does drive himself in his red (what other colour would he choose?) Ferrari. He ostentatiously shows off his opulence (absolutely no innuendoes intended whatsoever!) and one of the girls will usually go home with him and no doubt earn a packet for a one night stand : that is if he's capable of a one night stand which I think is exceedingly unlikely! He cannot hold his drink (despite being educated in Australia—hey, possums, what the bloody hell went wrong with his education I wonder?) and invariably ends up pretty ratted. Of course, everything is on the house for him (though he likes to pretend he is paying for everything) but definitely not for his friends (well, those he calls his friends but who are really hangers-on)—I draw the line at that. When his father comes—very occasionally—of course I give him the real royal treatment as I do when the Beijing officials pop in. My girls do as well of course! (They've been well-trained/brought up.) It's called keeping the customer satisfied. Their wives never show up here, of course, but they still get together at my restaurant from time to time—great little 'hen' nights they sometimes have together. Still freebies for them of course! It's called keeping the customer satisfied. Rarely, if ever, see their husbands there with them though.

As I said, last time not sure what my next venture will be.

Oh, by the way, the grapevine has it that Peter as he likes to call himself (real name Zhang Zie) has been asked to contribute his views on China today for this volume of prose to be sent to some Indian wallah who wrote to Wen Jiabao. Well, trust me, if that is the case his contribution must be being ghosted : he still hasn't got a vocabulary of words of more than two syllables so how the hell he can even tell you he was educated (Zhen De?) in Australia I don't know. What a fucking joke!

Australia? . . . . nah!

India? . . . . now there's a thought!

JENNY JING

A h, yes, it's vitally important my daughter gets a good education so I pay for her to go to a boarding school just outside of Beijing. You didn't know we had private schools? But of course we do. Oh, they're not such spectacular campuses, nor do they have such wonderful facilities as the famous English Public Schools (only the English would call private schools 'public' wouldn't they? And they question China referring to itself as a communist state!) Nor do they have the small class sizes which are a feature of those schools. But, dare I suggest, our students even in class sizes of 40 plus get as good, if not better results than their English counterparts. By the way, I have every intention of making sure my daughter can take English school qualifications when she gets to High School so she can attend a good university either in the UK or USA. Again, this is possible for our children here in China. No, they cannot attend the vastly overpriced and even more vastly overrated international schools which have mushroomed here in the last few years thanks to our opening up policy (unless you're a dual passport holder, that is) but there are ways within our own schools of setting up international courses. This is China—you can get and do anything you want . . . . at a price of course. In the great 1.3 billion food chain of the National Government Education Committees, the local, provincial Government Education Committees, the Principals and Party Secretaries of local High, Middle and Primary schools, the teachers . . . . etc Again, I am sure you get the picture! Why do I want her to go abroad to study? Well, I myself managed two years studying at Liverpool University getting an MBA. What an experience that proved to be.

Academically it was OK. No! Better than OK. Very good indeed. But the social experience of the city opened my eyes. Here's us only recently coming out of the rather dark, troubled and violent times of the Cultural Revolution and Liverpool and some other cities I visited seem to be going into them or at least a decidedly English variant of them. One in three of the derelict terraced houses up by Anfield housed squatters and druggies (well, what goes around comes around—remember the opium wars?) and the schools nearby had more used needles chucked in the playground than you would find in the waste bins of the A & E section of the local hospital. When Liverpool entertained some teams in the Premiership—especially Arsenal, Manchester United, Chelsea and Everton the city seemed under siege. When Everton entertained some teams in the Premiership—especially Arsenal, Manchester United, Chelsea and Liverpool the city also seemed under siege! I also thought the idea of the English as lager louts only really occurred on the continent when England or the English were playing in some cup winners' cup winners' cup winners' cup winners' cup or whatever but the weekend nights in the city (and not just the weekend nights!) proved me wrong on that. All a bit frightening to us Chinese.

I say 'us' because thankfully there were quite a few Chinese students on the same course as me and we decided there was safety in numbers so we kept ourselves to ourselves most of the time. Thankfully too, there's a large ex-pat Chinese community in Liverpool—the largest outside London I believe—so we made some friends there and it was good to get some 'home' cooking as most Chinese restaurant fare in the UK shall we say leaves much to be desired! Even the dog doesn't really taste like dog! There are big connections of course between Liverpool in its heyday when it flourished as a trading seaport and ship building city and Shanghai which, of course, continues to flourish big time as a trading seaport and shipbuilding city. They say there's a copy of the Liver Building in Shanghai but I've never seen it when I've been to Shanghai though it's clear The Bund area is modelled to a certain extent on the Liverpool docks area. Pity no

so I know Liverpool is John Osborne's 'red brick' university idea—it really is academically impressive.

Back to my history. When I got back from the UK I met and married Whang Hui, a local TV producer with Xinhua News Agency. Within just over a year, I gave birth to our lovely daughter, LaLa. For the next 3 years our marriage was idyllic. My parents looked after LaLa and we were able to carry on with our careers. Hui got promotion and I was doing very good deals not least with the help of Zhang Xiaobo (more of him later) so we were doing very nicely thank you. Unfortunately, I found that Hui was endeavouring to live the life more appropriate to that of the former Chinese emperors. Yes, he was having affairs at work and even frequenting places like Houhai and Sanlitun with their well known places of ill repute. I had to tackle him about this and he went on about needing comfort women given my cold responses to him. Comfort women! How I hate that term and how I hate those type of women in our society. Yes, I know they are there and I know they are in every society. But that's the fault of men. They seem to want to have new or different women just as we women want a new pair of shoes! I really do hate that—them wanting new women, not us wanting new shoes! And how dare he say I was cold towards him? Why couldn't Hui just want me and want to stay at home in the evenings? I was always there for him. Sure I was very tired most of the time as my job was quite demanding but . . . . Oh, why am I telling you all of this?

We got a divorce. Getting a divorce is not as difficult as it used to be in China. Many of my friends are divorced. Some are separated from their husbands which is the same things as far as I am concerned though they won't always admit that. Thankfully I have custody of LaLa and anyway, Hui did not contest this issue. Anyway he did not seem very disposed to visiting her or seeing her very often so that suits me and my family fine. I managed to get her a place at a weekly boarding school as you know and things have gone along swimmingly though I have to admit I was pretty devastated during the divorce. Used to listen to endless, sad love songs and cry myself to sleep. But then, thank goodness for Oprah Winfrey and her programme with its excellent advice and its encouragement for women to be strong, that's what I say. She helped me rally round and pull myself together. Oh, yes, we get her out here on The Hallmark Channel now called Diva Universal—what's in a name?—every weekday night from 8.00p.m.—9.00p.m. and then there's sometimes extended broadcasts of her special feature programmes! A real life saver as far as I was concerned.

BILL

I've told you how to get round in China. Here's the first instalment of how to get by. Actually, it's a kind of preparation for getting by. An induction, let's say. And a good induction at that!

I apologise to those who feel what I am about to write is sexist. But then as an author I assert my right to be identified as the author of this work asserted in accordance with Section 77 of the Copyright, Designs and Patent Act 1988 and I am a male . . . . and in this case you'll just have to believe that as my medical records are strictly private. If there is a woman who wishes to write a complementary article on behalf of women, please contact Wen Jiabao or his secretary, Sheng Yapin.

There are massage parlours and massage parlours. After reading this you can decide which type I have experienced/I am writing about. Anyway, massage parlours are generously spread throughout the highways and byways of the cities and, although they do not exactly gaudily advertise their presence in bright, flashing, giant neon lights or with monster posters or giant arrows stating 'This Way To Massage(e)' in Chinese or English, or with a myriad of silk-clad ladies and/or suited men who form the guards of honour at Karaokes or restaurants, it doesn't exactly need or take a Sherlock Holmes to find them. (But beware of what is advertised in this way e.g. KTV studios—there are massage parlours and massage parlours; right?)

Having found one, the entrance, generally discretely guarded behind thick, draped curtains, is usually the size of a cinema foyer and the reception desk like some western saloon bar. Approach and pay and give up your shoes. Yes, shoes. Just your shoes . . . . at this stage! If you haven't come across this custom on entering a Chinese house yet, you really have lived a terribly sheltered existence in the People's Republic of China! In turn you will receive a locker key and a pair of fresh slip-on, disposable mules which are almost as plentiful as chopsticks in China. Saunter over to your locker and strip off. Everything! Now wearing only the mules and locker key in its rubber wrist band approach phase one where your pair of fresh slip-on, disposable mules which are almost as plentiful as chopsticks in China are discarded as you enter the wash area.

Power shower time! And sauna and/or steam bath time. Indulge. The shampoos and shower gels are fragrant, the saunas and steam baths really tone you up. The foot baths are positively aromatic (though the brown-tea colour can be a bit off putting.) Cleanse that body, every bit of it, and then let the men cleanse you further before proceeding. Yes men! There are massage parlours and massage parlours; right?

You now know you are taking part in a ritual. Something akin to a religious one. Cleansing is a key part of it. Spread eagled on the elevated table the men will dry you off like you have never been dried before. (If you are blushing at that statement then you have already forgotten this chapter is about massage parlours and not massage parlours.) You really didn't believe they could make towels with the texture of really rough sandpaper, did you? In the hands of these men, that's what the towels now feel like. Putting your nose—and not just your nose—to the grindstone becomes literally true and not just metaphorically so. They don't actually remove your epidermis, though at times that what it feels like is happening. Surely you feel you must be bright lobster red from the abrasions that must be appearing on your skin. But, no, finally you are thoroughly dried off outside and inside out and as white (or as tanned) as ever. Not a drop of moisture now exists on your frame (not even a drop of blood!)—drier than any spray or roll-on deodorant dares claim to make and/or keep you.

Pain. You have felt the initial pain. Religious ritual now becomes a journey. Dying from one state into another. A spiritual one and it involves further pain in order to be thoroughly cleansed. Stage one completed, you enter phase two.

You are re-robed. Old clothes, used towels have been discarded and now the old body must also be thoroughly erased. So now you are clad anew in laundry-clean, loose fitting pyjamas with knee length bottoms akin to baggy Bermuda shorts and yet another pair of those ubiquitous, fresh, slip-on, disposable mules which are as about as plentiful as chopsticks in China. This makes you feel better and you start to forget your towel tormentors, the scourers who have remained mute throughout their service, perhaps sworn to a vow of silence—it would certainly be in keeping with the ambience of the place. Only the gentle splashing water and the hissing of steam can ever be heard in the background as you move out of phase two, onwards and upwards into the ante chamber for the all-important phase three.

Others lounge around here, similarly clothed like yourself. Now you see and start to feel you are at one with them and they with you. You gain confidence : you are not alone on this journey. You recall the play of *Everyman*. "Everyman, I will go with thee, to be thy guide : In thy most need to be by thy side." But you fail to remember these are the words of his avowed companion who conveniently buggers off as he dies—What does the song say : "You left me, just when I needed you most!"! Here you relax, as if, like Christian, you have reached The Delectable Mountains, having come through The Slough of Despond. You imagine the postcard you'd write . . . . "I've arrived at a great place but had a hell of a time getting here . . . ." forgetting that The Castle of Giant Despair and The Valley of The Shadow of Death and more are still to come. You may drink here, eat here, smoke even. You start to feel comfortable again. This place is deliberately soporific. The subdued silence, however, remains. The respite is short lived as you are conducted by a gorgeous lady (to prevent any outbreaks of fear and trembling) to phase three.

Through heavy curtains into a darkened room. There are small fairy lights—a bit like the corridor guiding lights on an aeroplane.—along the heavily carpeted corridors between the tables, just sufficient to guide you with the help of the gorgeous lady to your personal elevated table. She motions you to take off the fresh, slip-on, disposable mules which are as about as plentiful as chopsticks in China, get on the table and lie flat on your back. No words are ever spoken : none are necessary. There is a small stool beside your table where another gorgeous lady will shortly sit and as the first gorgeous lady departs, you await the arrival of the second. The one who will be your personal masseuse. As you wait, your eyes adjust to the dimness and you hear the occasional sounds of fists pummelling skin and hands slapping legs and feet and all parts of human bodies, just like yours, lying out on the couches. Despite the obvious physical torment these sounds imply, there are no screams—only these noises, and these alone, occasionally break the subdued, darkened silence of the place. You do not look around, just straight up, awaiting your own fate which you know now to be inexorable. You are now one of the souls about to join the souls in agony around you.

And as you look up a beautiful face comes in to view. It looks down at you and smiles. Not the masochistic, smirky smile of a torturer, but a genuine, red-lipped, inviting smile, and shiny lips you want to kiss, like Romeo when he first meets Juliet. You do stir slightly, enough to see she is clad in a soft, silk blouse, Chinese style, of course, and black trousers. She is carrying a bottle of baby oil. And she looks gorgeous. Silky. Beautiful. Attractive. A genuine Pearl of the Orient. Just like in the films. Just like you have always dreamed of. The devil, indeed, has many disguises. Fortunately, she does not break your initial fantasy by saying something crass like, "Hi! I'm Linda, and I'm your masseuse for the evening. Have a nice massage(e)." She quietly just places the bottle of oil within her reach, moves the stool and takes up her first position behind your head. You close your eyes . . . .

Although you have probably worked out how far up your nose you can stick your finger, you have never really considered, or known come to that, how far the human finger could penetrate inside the human ear, have you? Now you find out. You also have probably never really considered, or known come to that, the number of erogenous zones on your face, have you? Now you find out. You feel every finger movement traced, prodded, squeezed, pinched into your face and just at the point where it may seem unbearable, the fingers soothe and relax you. The torture is exquisite—you hope it will last!

And it doesn't just last, it develops. Satisfied that your skull covering needs no more treatment, it's on to shoulders and arms, elbows, wrists and fingers. More kneading, squeezing, pinching, prodding and when your fingers are individually dealt with and stretched with a resounding whip-like crack as they are violently released by your masseuse, you wonder if they are broken and will you ever hold a pen (or anything come to that) with them again. Equally, when your arms are treated like lengths of rubber tubing and flicked so that they give a wave trace which could be comfortably monitored on an oscilloscope giving a reading in the region of the order of a minor earth tremor, you wonder if you have always been double, nay triple or quadruple jointed but had never realized it.

And now a gentle tap on top of your head motioning you to sit up. Followed by a gentle tap on the chest motioning you remove your pyjama top. You readily comply mainly now because you are resigned to the inevitable. There is no escape. Grin and bear it. Stiff-upper lip, and all that. Yes lip! The top is taken from you, you are motioned to lie back again (and think of England or China or something asexual for Chrissake!) as oil is now delicately poured over your chest and rubbed in by those sensual hands and fingers. The hands and fingers now slide smoothly over your shoulders, your neck, your chest, your stomach, your . . . . how far can she go? That's for her to decide and you to find out. But please remember, as stated at the start, I am writing about massage parlours here, not massage parlours.

And so onto the legs, ankles, toes, soles of the feet. You have heard how police and prison warders are adept at using rubber truncheons to beat up prisoners in their cells and yet leave not a mark on their body. She doesn't use, she doesn't even need rubber truncheons. Skilled in using her fists and her hands in rapid punching and slapping movements, you feel you must be covered in internal contusions which must be making your legs, ankles, toes and soles of your feet black and blue. She also doesn't use, doesn't even need bamboo sticks (even though they are as ubiquitous as chopsticks and those fresh, slip-on, disposable mules) with which to beat the soles of your feet. The fists fly in and the punches would do justice to Mike Tyson or Evander Holyfield or Lennox Lewis or whoever Don King has decided is the current heavyweight champion of the world. The pain is unbearable, you hope it won't last.

And it doesn't. Just at the point of confessing everything (even though you're not sure what it is you must confess) or like Winston Smith screaming out to O'Brien, "Do it to Julia! Do it to Julia!" in *1984* you are now initially assaulted by warm, very warm, steaming even, towels being placed over all the parts of your body previously dealt with. Now, along with the abrasions and bruises, you feel you will bear scald marks for ever and begin to entertain illusions about claiming damages . . . . if you come out of this alive, that is. Then you remember you are in China where civil redress is not a legalistic possibility : it is only an idea in your mind. (Like 2 + 2 = 4.) But, yet again there's not a mark on your body—so just try proving it! You are now motioned to turn over. "For this relief, much thanks." Short lived though it is.

Now lying face down, there is a porthole size hole in the couch allowing you to look downwards at the floor—visions of Tom Cruise in the hospital scene in *Born on The Fourth of July* cloud the mind now at times in this position—and you occasionally see your masseuse's red-painted toe-nails as she circumnavigates the head of the couch and begins work over again. Seemingly not quite as intensively, the neck, shoulders, arms, legs and feet are all dealt with before the final piece de resistance. You have come to know what to expect on these features of your body and so the shock of second phase treatment is not as great as the first.

But now. The oil again. Poured delicately onto your back. Ahhhhhhhh, so soothing. It gives a new meaning to the scientific term, 'viscosity.' And better is yet to come. Looking resolutely at the floor, trying to erase the Tom Cruise vision, you feel an initial hiatus. Where has she gone? And suddenly, she has mounted the couch, her knees astride your buttocks and her fingers, hands and her arms, almost her whole upper clothed body seems to rub the oil luxuriously over and into, into and down your back. How far can she go? That's for her to decide and you to find out. But please remember, as stated at the start of this chapter, I am writing about massage parlours here, and not massage parlours. Then there's her knee thrust right into the small of your back. Agggghhhhhhhhhhhhhhhhhhh . . . . it can go off the end of the page. What's her nick-name? Bone crusher? Spine-crusher? And then release. This was worth waiting for. Sweet is the pleasure after pain!

Consummatum est? Oh no, not quite.

Another brief hiatus as she gets off and you get the warm, very warm, steaming even, towel treatment again across all the back parts of your body this time of course. These are removed and then finally . . . .

To dry that bruised, battered and bewildered back of yours, a dry towel is placed across it and she gets up on the couch again, this one last time and by caressing your back between her knees (that's a euphemism) and by gently moving up and down, she dries you off. Yes dries. It was, indeed, worth all the suffering, the agony, the pain, the crazy legal redress illusions, the visions of Tom Cruise even . . . .

That's it. She helps you on with the previously discarded top and your fresh, slip-on, disposable mules which are as about as plentiful as chopsticks in China and gently shows you the way out.

Who needs massage parlours when you can get all this in massage parlours?

As you head out to the apres treatment room and a brief time of recuperation following such a spiritually uplifting experience you start to muse. (Yes, spiritually uplifting!) Others, similarly clad who have been through the treatment like yourself and survived and maybe reached Nirvanah are there too and they are probably musing too. But faces are implacable and inscrutable. There is no indication from them, or from you (at least you hope) of what you were or are thinking. And as you lounge and drink or eat or even smoke during this period of convalescence you muse further.

She looked only 17, 18 or 19 or only in her early twenties at most. Where did she learn this incredible art? Do they have Massage Therapy centres at their Colleges of F.E. like the Beauty Therapy centres in the Colleges of F.E. in the U.K.? Well do they? And who are the lucky bastards they get to practise their skills on for free whilst completing their post 16 or post 18 diploma or whatever? Better still, who are their examiners? Better still again, could you apply to be one? You'd be more independent than the Chinese examiners. These musings fade and you enter into a more relaxed frame of mind and reflect.

Yes, it was sensual and sexual and they know that as well as you. But it wasn't a fantasy, it was for real. But how about developing the fantasy? What must it be like to marry or be the partner of one of these wonderful, gorgeous women? Your imagination runs wild again. You could get this treatment every night of the week. Aggghhhhhhhhhhhhh . . . . it could go off the end of the page.

As you sit she walks past you, heading who knows where? Her original, welcoming and beckoning smile is still there. Those red, inviting, Romeo-tempting lips. It's not the satisfied, masochistic grin of a torturer who has extracted the confession. Nor the insightful smile suggesting she now knows more about you than you hoped to disclose. Just a warm, oriental, inviting, tempting smile. You smile back. Every night of the week . . . .? Every night of the week? Every night . . . .

Reality hits you as you exit where you came in, this time handing over your locker key and exchanging your fresh, slip-on, disposable mules which are about as plentiful as chopsticks in China for your shoes. These women are like the top chefs. When they go home, they're too tired to cook so they stick something in the microwave.

FU

Ladywork in Shanghai. That's what we call it. A euphemism, of course, but a nice one. Oh, come on; I am sure you worked out what I do from my earlier innuendoes, you're not that ignorant a reader—how else would I have known all those references? (PBUH, Oscar Wilde etc . . . . remember now? I am sure you do.) How else would I have learned the use of the vernacular I know? Yes I have had quite a few men or should I say quite a few men have had me. Eleanor really was as good as her word—we got our dinner and drinks but they were hardly 'free'. Well, they were in a kind of way—we certainly didn't have to pay, at least not in cash. But then nor did she! Oh, and we even got paid as well as getting the food and drink. The Long Bar, being in the Shanghai Centre where the Portman Ritz Carlton was and very adjacent to The JC Mandarin and just up the road from The Four Seasons Hotel . . . . well there were no end of rich clients. And, over and above those, there was always the football crowd in to watch their premier league action (which they could of course get a variant of in practice from us had they so wished .... for an entrance fee naturally!) on the big screen on Saturdays and Sundays—always late on, of course, because of the time differences.

O.K. It's easy to criticize me and the likes of me but it's important to understand what we do even if that doesn't excuse, to you, what we do. We are part of social services. We provide a much needed and most welcome social service to our clients. We act just like the counselors you seem to call in after any situation big or small that you consider in some ways traumatic to any of the participants or any on lookers. Our men are often here on brief business trips or sometime just on limited contracts for two, maybe three years. They are often very lonely in this big city where they don't speak or read the language and life in hotel rooms or apartment blocks, cooped up maybe with other ex-pats is not exactly thrilling. Their jobs are stressful and they need to relax. What better way than in bed in the arms of an attractive young lady? It's not necessarily the fact that they are pissed off with their wives and their home/family lives : it's not at all the 'my wife doesn't understand me' syndrome, no way! Often it is quite clear that they love and adore their wives and families all dearly but, being away from them, they need to unwind, to get rid of some of their frustrations just to have a comfortable and enjoyable time. We provide a familiarity that they desperately need—a bit like Burger King, MacDonalds, KFC . . . . though I rather consider myself Starbucks or Costa rather than being just a fast food variety. I guess in current Chinese terms I should consider myself Element Fresh or Wagas!

From what I gather, what we do here is very different—well if not very different at least at one or two or more removes—from what hookers or whatever you call them do in the Western world. There they are often into kinky sex, bondage, sex toys and the like. Yes, there are sex shops here and occasionally, very occasionally, I have heard tales of such demands on the likes of me and my friends. But that's really most unusual and we would all hope to avoid that sort of engagement. We are into quiet, calm, reposeful evenings. Chatting to our male companions, enjoying drinks and nice food and then sauntering back via taxi or, if they are near to the Long Bar, just walking to their hotel rooms or their apartments and spending the night with them. No, they do not come home with us. We get the best of their worlds—I've been in the best hotels and the best apartment blocks in this city of magnificent hotels and apartment blocks believe me. I've also been in some of the best hotels in some of the best foreign holiday spots in the world. I've had some terrific foreign holidays—Bali, Singapore, The Phillipines, Thailand, Malaysia, Hong Kong, Macau and, most recently, places I thought once I would only see in my dreams—London, Paris, Milan and Rome!

Yes we get paid. Dare I say handsomely, indeed? Who doesn't charge for his/her services? I may be part of social services but I'm not a charity! Truly handsomely as a matter of fact. On average I earned (please note the tense!) 28,000RMB to 32,000RMB a month. A bit better than what I got from China Telecom, I think you'll agree! Indeed, I earned (please note the tense) more than many women my age earn in a year . . . . untaxed naturally! Well sort of. To be fair, Eleanor never took a cut though we, her 'girls' did look after her (and still do now she's doing time, silly girl!) but Matthew, the bar manager, required a payment for our presence and always, of course, encouraged us to get the punters to buy the most expense drinks. We didn't have to do much to encourage them. They always seemed keen to impress us so they would flash the cash—well, often it was expenses anyway so what did they care? We had regulars, naturally. That was good for us and good for them. They would know that on their trips we were always there to service their needs. And they would bring us lovely gifts from their home countries. Sometimes we could even give them a personal shopping list before they left!

These were some of the perks but there were plenty more closer to home. I once saw a T shirt (and I really wish I'd bought it) that had the caption emblazoned on it : "Take me shopping and I'll pretend to be your girl-friend." That's exactly what it's like. They love being seen out with investment for my future. I have life assurance policies, pension policies—I have invested well and so have my many friends in this business. I have membership of the best gym and Yoga Club in the city (I am in fact a qualified yoga instructor—did the course but I never paid for it of course!) and gym membership of one of the best gyms in the city. Well, must keep myself fit and looking the part! I'm now also attending a Spanish language course : well, you never know when I might make it to Madrid, Toledo or Seville! Or maybe meet a nice Spanish gentleman! (I guess all of that now sounds a lot like one of your nouveau riche 60's pop stars or one of the 21st century over paid Premiership footballers!)

It's a great life if you don't weaken . . . . but, in a kind of way I have weakened. (Perhaps we all do?) Not too seriously but there comes a time when one has to consider one's future, doesn't one? To be honest, enjoyable though this life can be there's a flat and dull side to it as well as there is to everything of course. Having affairs with quite a few men is all very well but there's no real deep and meaningful relationship involved. It's all a bit objective, a bit clinical, a bit insubstantial, a bit distant really. How I always longed for something more meaningful. Sometimes when I was with a client, maybe even a regular one, in my mind I was many miles away. I was going through the motions, enjoying myself certainly and getting all

WU DABIN &
JIANG SHULIN

Dear Mr Harding

We wish to thank you most sincerely for providing the funding to allow our daughter, Dongdong, to take the trip to the UK and to study for one month at the Camera School of English in Cambridge this coming summer. We are sure she will enjoy the experience and make the most of it and it will certainly help her improve her command of the English language which in turn will stand her in good stead when she takes the gao kao next year. I am sure she will be able to thank you personally when she returns and she will be able to tell you about how she got on and how much she enjoyed visiting England.

We would also like to take this opportunity of thanking you for being such an excellent employer for me at the school and for my wife as your ayi. You

really are kind and generous and you are a nice person
and god will bless you, we are sure.

Yours sincerely

Wu Dabin & Jiang Shulin

JENNY JING

Zhang Xiabo. Remember I mentioned him? I'm sure you do. What a great help he was in developing my realty work. O.K. so he's regarded as the mad Chinaman who built the stunning (hardly the right word but I don't want to offend him since he was and is so good to me) copy of Neuschwanstein castle on the outskirts of Beijing. A definite tourist spot on the landscape even if most just spend a few minutes gasping in awe at it. (Am I in China? Am I in Germany? Where the fuck am I?) Being a government official he gave me all the introductions I needed to get licences for development of shopping malls, international schools, golf-driving ranges, residential compounds etc. And I didn't have to give him any favours in return . . . . except cash in hand and keeping his name out of any deals of course. Anonymity is very much part of the game in deals here. But best of all, he introduced me to his son, Zhang Xie, who calls himself Peter. What a thick idiot that boy (he's hardly a man) is! How his wise father ever let him work in his business, gave him responsibilities even, I really don't know. It's Peter who is the mad Chinaman (Australian? Since he does go on about being educated—what a fucking joke—there!) not his father, let me assure you.

Well, the great thing about working with Peter is he is so dumb (he really should have been a blonde!) that you can get anything past him. So it was he had been approached by some even dumber Americans who wanted to open up an international school on his land next to the castle. Peter hadn't a clue about how to deal with this, probably would have signed up to allowing it immediately had I not intervened because I saw the opportunities for some ready bucks. So I got him to do the usual i.e. act the pleasant host routine—Chinese dinner cum banquet at the Neuschwanstein Castle cum hotel initially. Subsequently give them a contract related to green sites which then could not possibly be honoured under Chinese law, get a down payment of $1,500,000 up front paid into a specially created legal entity account in a Chinese bank, have a contract (a snapshot of a set of arrangements that happen to exist at the time as far as Chinese law is concerned) and sit back until their patience (or should I say impatience?) starts to get the better of them. When it does, string them along for a little while longer before reneging on the deal because of Chinese law. The deposit? Non-refundable, of course! Anyway, by that time the specially created legal him, of course) I am pleased to say. No doubt he liked his backhander of $250,000 as well! And he and Peter have had a bit more to add to this since, from deals I've made. Got to keep them sweet! You give a little love and it all comes back to you! Well, not love exactly! Through them both I have got to know Michelle Wong, the owner of two of the most notorious nightclubs in the city! She's a very bright and able business women and although I don't approve of the places she owns (though Kuaizi, the restaurant is OK I suppose, though I guess it's a front in a way for all the hanky panky in the clubs and is useful for money laundering!) I admire what she has achieved. Us business women/ entrepreneurs must stick together.

Mind you I envy her her Hong Kong citizenship and UK passport as it enables her to send her daughter to Lancing College International school here in the city. That's a big plus for sure. I haven't managed to circumnavigate that aspect of the law laid down by our government yet in favour of my daughter and don't expect I (or anyone else) ever will. The best we can look forward to are the international set ups for UK/American exams in our second rate universities, some Chinese state schools or some of our private schools. Well, they get the results there but it's not quite the same, is it? There's no lovely blazers or school uniform making the students look fashionable and smart, no activities programmes and sports fixtures and the facilities are pretty low grade by comparison. Not quite in the league of the old school tie network that operates in the UK and which now seems to apply to their satellite international set ups like Lancing.

I mustn't grumble really. Even though I can't send my daughter there I have made money from the Lancing International School set up. As they expanded so they needed premises on two of the compounds I had been fortunate to work on with the developers. I was happy to do the deals for them of course. I was even happy to get Tsui Haibin, a close architect friend of my ex, involved. He's a really nice guy and has become an even closer friend of mine recently. There was another 'insult' in pay off terms from Lancing of course but I look upon it as a kind of re-cycling in the economy. Western money being put into China but coming back to Chinese people in Chinese currency. A reasonable merry-go-round.

I, in turn, recycle that money so westerners cannot really grumble either. Last year I managed to take a trip to the USA with Lala. We did a kind of grand tour—San Francisco, Las Vegas, Death Valley, New Orleans, Nashville, Memphis—including Grace Lands, of course—New York, Boston, Orlando and Disneyland naturally!—it was delightful. This year Tsui Haibin is taking me to Hawaii. Yes, I suppose you could say we are 'an item' or at least we are rapidly becoming one! I am so looking forward to that trip, believe me. Lala will not be with us. Adults do need some quality time on their own after all. She is going on a course to the Camera School of English in Cambridge (such a lovely city!) which I hope will pay dividends for her in her ability to master the English language and will get her good marks in her school when she takes her exams in the future. I am also sure she will meet an equally favourable class of international students there and therefore make some excellent friends for life. (Or if she doesn't make excellent friends I sincerely hope she will make useful ones—those are the real kind of friends to have as I have found from my life so far.) Moreover, it really will be good for her to be away from her mother's apron strings for a while though I know she will be fretting about me just as I will about her.

PETER

You know I never get fed up with reciting that story about those dumb Americans. The girls I meet in Den of Iniquity love it. In fact the girls I meet anywhere and everywhere love it! Adds to my attraction though to be honest I don't need that added to as I'm attractive enough already for sure.

Yes I have plenty of girls but as I also said I have what I call my occasional family. I am a married man actually. My wife's a real beauty. Stunning, I should say! She's Thai, her name's Susie and I have two children by her. I met her in Patpong Market in Bangkok. It was love at first sight. There I was happily enjoying a brew in one of the many bars in one of the delightful and colourful clubs along the Patpong strip when I saw this gorgeous, golden tanned lady strutting her stuff on the catwalk. She noticed I couldn't keep my eyes off her and came straight over to me once she's done her dance along with the others. I bought her a drink, naturally and we got talking. She told me she's been Miss Bangkok just a couple of years' back and went on to be runner up as Miss Thailand just failing to qualify for the Miss South East Asia finals. She certainly looked the part, there's no getting away from that. Wow, I thought to myself, am I a lucky bugger or what?

As I said, it was love at first sight for me and so it was for her as she had no hesitation in coming away with me that very evening and acting as my 'guide' round that beautiful city for the next three days whilst I was holidaying there. I did, of course, give a generous tip to the manager of the bar before we left and Susie wisely encouraged me to do so : it was well worth it by the way as here I had met the love of my life. I also had no hesitation in getting married to her as she suggested before I was due to return to China—there's many places in the city where foreigners can marry Thais—and she was very anxious to come back to China with me which showed just how much she loved me. However, even though we were married she still had to get a visa so I promised to return to Bangkok to bring her back to China once she had obtained her visa. Before leaving I of course gave her some cash to tide her over until my return. Well, it was the husbandly thing to do, wasn't it?

On getting home initially I decided not to say anything to the olds. I thought it would be a great and happy surprise for them when I eventually brought her home. That, indeed, proved to be the case a few weeks

Thai names you wouldn't be able to cope!) aged 4 and 7 and they come over to see their grandparents once in a while as well. Mum and Dad love them both of course and spoil them when they see them but I get the feeling they would still wish for me to be married to a Chinese girl and have children by her. Well, it's not for want of trying on my part I can tell you for as I said I do have lots of girl-friends. However, in all honesty I have not met anyone as beautiful as my heart's darling, Susie. She has wanted me as much as I have always wanted her whereas the birds I pick up now seem to lose interest all too quickly. Can't think why as I treat them really well. And after all I fuck them, don't I?

Mum and Dad introduce me to some members of the opposite sex occasionally. Some very refined ladies indeed and some lookers from time to time. I know they are only trying to help though sometimes I wonder if it they're trying to help me or help themselves? I try to tell them I still love Susie and I am, after all a married man but they tell me the certificate I got in Thailand isn't worth the paper it's written on. Bit like a verbal agreement? (Get the joke?) A bit like that contract I made with those Americans I guess! Not sure whether to believe that or not really.

Anyway, life goes on. Love and marriage, girl-friends and all that are all very well but my priority rests in having to keep the family business going. Dad and I ain't getting any younger and long term I'll be in charge of the whole company. It's important in the meantime I do good deals and learn more about things if we are to be successful. Fortunately I have made some good contacts like Jenny Jing and Michelle Wong is a great friend.

Work hard and play hard, that's my motto. Meanwhile though with regard to my marriage to Susie, Mum and Dad . . . . ni bu dong wode xin.

BILL

Here's another starter for getting by. But this is a reputable one. Trust me, there's Karaoke studios and Karaoke studios. What's here is about Karaoke studios.

Who invented Karaoke : the Chinese or the Japanese? The Chinese. This is their country. End of story. Now let's get on.

Taking part in a Karaoke is just one of the ways to cement Sino-British relationships. Massage Parlours are another. Not the Massage Parlours previously described but Massage Parlours. Trust me just like Karaoke studios and Karaoke studios there's Massage Parlours and Massage Parlours and there is a relationship with Karaoke studios but not the ones I'm going to tell you about here. Yes, must get on.

Preparation for the evening out is very important.

Now, if you have been dragged in screaming to a Karaoke evening in the U K as a fund raiser at your Squash Club, School P T A or maybe at a charity event at a local pub or whatever, your preparation will have consisted of getting together with your mates, downing at least a gallon of *Carlsberg* or some such lager before arriving, tottering on stage after further imbibing at the pub or club, giving it atonal, x factor decibel renditions of *New York, New York, It's Not Unusual* or *My Way* and perhaps even doing with your mates (if they and you can still stand) a David Bowie/Mick Jagger impression and version of *Dancing in the Street* or, more likely, 'cause your so pissed, the Martha and Vandella's version, which you think is David Bowie and Mick Jagger—after all, you wouldn't be a ponce and sing a girlies' number, would you? *Christ, I was good*, you think to yourself as you puke up in the toilets a bit later. So good, indeed, you didn't realise how nervous it made you until after the event : that's really what has made you sick. Yes, you can hold your drink.

Unfortunately, this sort of preparation is definitely NOT on in China. Your Chinese friends take Karaoke relatively seriously and will expect you, up to a point at least, to do the same. Let's not insult them by saying Karaoke has become part of their culture : let us merely state it is part of their social activities and, as such, it means more to them than it could ever mean to you : unless, that is, you are desperately trying to get recommended for an audition for *Stars in Their Eyes*. Oops, sorry that reference is probably more relevant to those of my generation/a certain age shall we say. I guess X Factor, Britain's Got Talent, American Idol or whatever might mean a bit more to some of you. In which case, let's be honest, you're not really taking it seriously : you're just plain stupid! (Yes, it is true that quite a few Chinese have Karaoke decks/machines .... whatever they are called .... all plugged in and linked to their T V in their little homes so that they can sing around the screen after dinner but that doesn't make it part of their culture. Was *Chukky Egg* or *Munchman* which you had on your home Commodore computer part of the U K culture? O.K. so you're into WII now, IPad 2, Angry Birds—big fucking deal!)

Your preparation, therefore, starts with your group. You will know the number of your host's party and you should try to equal that number or at least be within no less than two of it. Usually, a good total size for a party is around 12, six in each is comfortable, more than that and you might all get booked as the chorus in *South Pacific* or *Miss Saigon* or *Madame Butterfly* or *Turandot* or *The King and I* or who knows? Ages are important, too. Try to have a least TWO members of your party who are in their very late thirties, early forties or better still, forties plus. They will at least have a chance of remembering The Carpenters, Roy Orbison, Glen Campbell, The Beatles, The Everley Brothers, Simon and Garfunkel, Roger Whittaker (Roger who???) and the like and may even remember the ballad,

"Tell Laura I love her," even if, like me, they have forgotten the name of the singer who recorded it. UB40, Guns 'n' Roses, Led Zepplin, Dire Straits, The Sex Pistols, Annie Lennox, Meatloaf, Nirvanah, Green Day and the like don't exactly lend themselves to a Karoake evening's entertainment and Freddie Mercury and Elton John are, as I am sure you will understand, highly inappropriate. Try also to get at least one person, even if he or she has to be Welsh, who can sing reasonably in tune.

So you meet up with your Chinese counterparts outside the building in which is the designated Karaoke studio. Smiles and handshakes all round and you are shitting yourself because you possibly have only had a chance to have one or maybe two, or perhaps even no drinks at all with your party beforehand. You are, to all intents and purposes, stone cold sober and you are going to a Karaoke evening. You didn't believe that was possible, did you? And, if you told your friends back home, they wouldn't believe you and they are never going to believe you anyway. This is one lie too far! Now you know what nerves are really like!

So, in you all go.

A simply splendid guard of honour awaits. To your left, teenage girls, suitably attired in brightly coloured silk dresses (with the side slit, of course) and to your right teenage boys, suitably attired in brightly coloured suits (without the side slit, of course.) The girls look attractive but are probably 'jail bait' and the boys look positively ridiculous. It's all a bit dazzling and their huge smiles indicate they have absolutely no idea of the agonies you are putting yourself through. As far as they are concerned, you, like their Chinese comrades, have come for a really great evening's entertainment : that's what your entitled to, since you're paying the money, and that's what you're going to get, whether you bloody well like it or not. Just think of it like the entitlement curriculum in schools. You have to run this gaudy gauntlet as you enter. You can almost hear the voice booming out announcing you like players in the N F L as they run on to the field. All that's missing here is the actual voice booming out the announcement, a massive crowd, the pompom girls and loads of music and razzmataz . . . . but you can imagine all that. It will help you on your way.

You are now led down brightly lit corridors, passing various sized rooms most with closed doors and through the tinted glass windows you can see people singing (or that's what you hope they are doing with the microphone) but you cannot hear them—sound proofing is excellent—it has to be! Eventually you are shown into a cosy room of suitable size for your group. It has appallingly coloured pvc surround setees which complement the surround sound and screen. Invariably the lighting within is coloured and dim and there may even be some fake stained glass effect on the door window. The first impression is of a tart's boudoir but we are writing about Karaoke studios here and not about Karaoke studios. In the centre is a ginormous, glass topped coffee type table with a tiny ashtray on it and to the left is the electronic, computerised command consul with appropriate flashing coloured lights and the dreaded, extended cable bearing the microphone. On reflection it's a bit more like the inside of Doctor Who's *Tardis* if it wasn't for that ashtray!

Even if you are a computer buff, let one of your Chinese friends operate the consul. He or she is well-used to it.

However, you can now order drinks and nibbles just to calm those nerves so get another Chinese friend to advise you on what's available and get the order in sharpish. You will find your hosts ordering cokes whilst you order your beers. As you settle down, the nibbles (if you've bothered to order any) are brought in along with the drinks (which you have definitely ordered) and placed on the great coffee table. The first disappointment. Lagers, and you all ordered a couple each, come in the 330ml cans—so you've only just got about a pint's worth. To send for more so soon would be offensive and you'll be surprised, much to your chagrin, as the evening progresses how long the Chinese can make a soft drink last. So it's all about to start, and you are still stone cold sober.

Your Chinese counterparts will by now have sequenced in most of what they want to sing and then they will scroll through what's available in the English/American versions for your delectation and delight. It is now that the 'olds' in your party come into their own. Get them to view the what's available and, after consulting with you and jogging your memory of songs you may have heard your parents listen to when they were being sloppy, romantic and sentimental, or about to head out for a 60's or 70's party suitably but embarrassingly dressed of course, and which, until the advent of C D re-release/digital re-recorded, were only available on vinyl—was it 78s, 45s or 33s?—decide on what your choice is going to be. There's no need to select the lot at once, you can (and will) look again later in the evening because it's bound to drag on and you are bound to be asked for encores. Well, maybe not bound to be; let's say probably.

Let the session begin.

Usually, your hosts will have selected their best singer and he or she will start off by singing something in English. They just love to impress! You should be able to predict what this is going to be since it is bound to be related to some recently released blockbuster movie or some major, major hit by a really, really big, big international star, star. Celine Dion's "My heart will go on," is such a number and it has a major, pretentious transition towards the end—you know the reprise bit . . . "Near, far, w h e r e v e r y o u a r e . . . . ."—which the Chinese just love and can imitate very well since it almost gets close to solos in Chinese opera! So whilst your sipping—yes sipping—your lager, this kick starts the evening. It's done well (because it has probably been done 100+ times by whoever was singing it before) and at the end there's polite applause and smiles all round. So for good measure, it will be usually sung again. Don't they just love to impress? Can't get enough of a good thing! At the end, a smattering of applause and on goes the evening. Now your hosts will probably turn to a couple of Chinese songs, fairly harmless and non-descript before it's your turn.

At this stage you've probably sipped enough of your larger to be able, without offence, to order some more which gives to time to confer on how your side will start. So the drinks order's gone off and you're in a huddle just like the offence in the N F L. Now be subtle. Even though Taffy is desperate to sing and impress, restrain him or her. Gag him or her if you have to! Don't start like your hosts in playing your ace first. You all need to get confidence and you know that's not available by way of Dutch courage at this event so go for a song with a chorus. The Everley Brothers' *Bye Bye, Love* or even *Dream, Dream, Dream* could work, the former being the more preferable of the two since it's a bit bouncier and might just get you all in the party mood.

Or The Carpenters *Top of the World* also works equally well. The drinks arrive. You shove the microphone into the hands of the least suspecting poor bastard of your group and it's "Music, maestro, if you please!"

Whoever the unfortunate is who gets the microphone makes a faltering start but the chorus line soon comes and you all join in, raucous as can be, and this saves the day and he or she manages to keep going thereafter with appropriate help whenever the chorus comes around. You hide your initial embarrassment by deliberately messing up the words at times (though the cue line on the video does that for you without you trying at times) and childish giggling. Your hosts hide their embarrassment by listening to the messed up words at times and by childish giggling. To your amazement, you get through it in a manner of speaking and, since your throats now feel like the inside of a tram-driver's glove, you immediately grab and down your drinks. Now a solo number from one of you. Even though Taffy is still desperate to sing and impress, restrain him or her. Gag him or her if you have to. Since you now all realise you can make a prat of yourself at this and it doesn't really matter, one of you can easily render *Yesterday, Sounds of Silence, The Wonder of You, Walk away, please go* or whatever now. So far so good. In fact, you start to relax and you start to catch the party atmosphere. Back to your hosts.

In your more relaxed mood now you actually start to watch the videos and occasionally listen to the words of the songs—the Chinese ones initially that is. After all, the characters mean bugger all to you. In the first instance, you notice in the Chinese songs lots of repetition of key words : qin (heart) yanjing (eyes) wo ai ni (I love you) wode (my) nide (your) hen hao (lovely, very beautiful) shangxin (sad)—so you learn a bit of vocabulary. Almost about as much as you would learn from listening to The Beatles' She Loves You, With Love from Me to You etc. Invariably the songs are pathetically romantic about losing or winning a loved one and the only saving grace is occasionally a nice tune or the orchestration which can sometimes use the Chinese instruments like the er hu or the bamboo flute to good effect. So you might be able to use those immortal words about the song, "I like the backing" but hardly would you ever "Give eet foive." (Your 'olds' may be able to understand and explain those illusions—if not, look up *Juke Box Jury* on the Internet and/or find out who Pete Murray was—phone your Mum or your Dad, preferably your Mum, on your mobile if you really have to.)

Better still are the videos. Britain had *The Ealing Studios* (your 'olds' may be able to recall these), America still has *Hollywood* and even India has *Bollywood*. China does have a film industry but the acting is about as good as it was on *Dallas* (do you remember J R's wife, Sue

Ellen—how could she possibly get her words out through that lipstick?) *Crossroads* (Benny—don't make me laugh!) or *El Dorado* (shouldn't use that as it really would be grossly insulting) but made even funnier because invariably it is set with an epic background filmed in various parts of the vast country that is The Peoples Republic of China. Clearly there's a bit of subliminal advertising going on here! Wide, wide expanses of fertile plains and hillsides, massive, solid imperial doors and gateways, sumptious palaces, magnificent cloud-topped, snowy mountains, prancing horses, wild cataracts leaping in glory . . . . The singer and or his girl-friend cross the plains and hillsides, wander lonely as a cloud about the mountains but don't seem to suffer from frost-bite even, stroke and soothe the prancing horses, get nice photo opportunities in front of the cataracts and in the palaces and bashes his or her head and fists in despair against the massive, solid imperial doors and gateways. Tears abound, expressions are so OTT as to be more frightening and/or more impressive than the Chinese opera masks. It's super stuff. Don't they just love to impress!

Incidentally, mid-way through the evening, you have at last ungagged Taffy and even you are forced to admit that he or she has done a spectacular rendering of Roy Orbison's *Crying*—the Chinese just love this number as it fits the Karaoke emotively tearful mood perfectly—or his *Pretty Woman*—ah, that's so Chinese!—and your Chinese hosts realise you are not all prats and do have something to offer. They are a bit bemused by his or her accent though. (If Taffy is a *he*, hearing how high he can sing might give you and them some concern. You thought the last male castrati sang at the Vatican in the 1920s but you are now having serious doubts about that!) However, his or her rendition does give you 'brownie points' and evens the score up a bit in the evening as whole. You've also, to your own surprise, individually probably got through *Listen to the rhythm of the falling rain*, *Durham Town*, *Country Roads*, *Close to You*, *Daydream Believer* and a few others of similar ilk so you have done not too badly. It's a pity you didn't have Terry Wogan or Ken Bruce with you to do the introductions to these numbers, but you can't have everything and anyway, Radio 2, unlike Radio 1, doesn't have a road show—you should know that. Well, the 'olds' in your party will anyway.

You have noticed the odd slip in spelling, translation or just printing of the words on the screen, of course, but have not offended your hosts by pointing them out. They wouldn't believe you anyway, and certainly would not get them changed as it would involve diulian i.e. loss of face to you. This is Karaoke. The Chinese invented Karaoke. This is China.

Of course, your major, and final rendition just has to be, the great, the immortal, the classic as sung by that one and only Taffy, Tom Jones, (Jones the voice, that is), *Green Green Grass of Home*. You have been building up to this all evening and you now have a real head of steam on. Even the Chinese will join in with you on this one. Now, O.K. so some lines are a bit garbled . . . . "the old town home looks the same" . . . . "down the road I look and there runs Merry" . . . . "so I awake and look around me, at four black* walls that surround me" . . . . but this doesn't really matter. (*Haven't you been to a Chinese tea-house yet and had some *Earl Black* tea? Tastes like *Earl Grey*—but don't you dare tell them that!) But suddenly, since you know the words of this anyway, you pay far more attention to the video which you have not really been doing on the English songs up until now, only on the Chinese ones and you notice . . . . wide, wide expanses of fertile plains and hillsides, massive, solid imperial doors and gateways, sumptious palaces, magnificent cloud-topped, snowy mountains, prancing horses, wild cataracts leaping in glory . . . . The singer and his girl-friend cross the plains and hillsides . . . . what's all this got to do with the *Green, Green Grass of Home* for fuck's sake? This is Karaoke. The Chinese invented Karaoke. This is China.

And it's over. (No! Quickly gag Taffy again before he or she starts singing another Roy Orbison number—it's not on the consul anyway!) You are all smiles. In your case from relief, in their case from enjoyment. You got through it, you walk out through the corridors and take not a glance behind. The guard of honour, still grinning like Cheshire cats and as gaudy as ever, offer you final salutations as you exit. Your Chinese hosts quickly get in a few pictures at this point so they will always have the evidence of how you made prats of yourselves and you walk outside, shake hands and part company. Honours are in their favour—after all they had someone who could sing in English : did any of your lot sing in Chinese?—which is just right since you are wanting to establish good Sino-British relations you know you should always let the home side win.

Fortunately, China has developed a pub culture of sorts so you head off to the nearest one (even if it has to be the local Irish theme bar with extravagant prices) and individually drink about a gallon of Carlsberg, Tiger, Tsingdao, San Miguel, Guinness, Kilkenny or whatever . . . . anything will do for fuck's sake!

As you later puke up in the toilets, you think to yourself . . . . . "Please God, Buddha, Allah, Chairman Mao . . . . whoever is up there, please don't let the Chinese know about Line Dancing? . . . . What's that you say? Oh no! Did they invent that as well?"

WU DABIN & JIANG SHULIN

Mr Harding. Such a nice man . . . .

Yes, sure is, a nice man indeed.

Don't interrupt, dear! Yes, so nice. He's paid for our daughter to do an English course in the UK. Not just nice of him but kind of him as well. Can't thank him enough. Our daughter will soon be in her gao kao year (that's her last year at school before university) so it's important she gets good scores and especially in English. This will help her a great deal . . . .

Well as you know I am his ayi and he treats me very well . . . . .

He treats me well too, at work. Really very supportive. Great guy. Great boss.

Yes, OK, dear, we heard you. Well, as you know, ex-pats when they are abroad on their own like he is, need company. I'm not just talking about their colleagues at work, or their friends outside of work. I am talking about 'company' or, as we say in China, "Englishman (well, it

could be American, Australian, German .... whatever ....
but definitely not Japanese!) need Chinese wife." I believe
there's other euphemisms used in the past like "sleeping
dictionary" for example? Well, I am sure you know what
I mean .....

..... Xiao Wu! Take that knowing grin off your
face! ....

Yes, well, he has helped us, so we should help him. But
that's not easy. He's a very shy and quiet man and I am not
sure he would take kindly to such a suggestion. We will
need to consider the situation carefully and see what we
can do. In the meantime we'll just keep you up to date with
what's going on as we continue to press on with our work.

Wu Dabin, you can comment now .... you seemed
eager enough to get in on the conversation earlier on.

Well, yes, dear. O.K. The school continues to have its
ups and downs and Mr Harding continues to turn various
shades of purple now and then. I wouldn't have his job for
the world. There's been a few crises I have heard about and
they are not all created by the Chinese side.

Some of the staff evidently went to The British
Chamber of Commerce Ball—it's a big do in the city
annually—a throw back to the 30s in my opinion.
Decadent and expensive and they are waited on head, hand
and foot by us Chinese as if nothing had changed and they
are still numero uno in world dominance terms! What a

fucking joke! Go tell that to the Americans . . . . or, better still indeed, us, the Chinese! Well, one of the members of staff who is Scottish turned up in his skirt—kilt I believe is what you call it—what are men doing wearing skirts? Are they gay or something? (I was told if you asked that of a Scot you'd get a Glasgow kiss—so I reckon they must be gay! Or am I missing something here?) Anyway, the usual question was asked . . . . What is worn under the kilt? (Naething! It's all in perfect, working order!—Sorry, that's a joke so I've been told.) Well, Jock Strap, or whatever the teacher's name is, decided to give a demonstration—not just to his colleagues at his table but to the guests at large. He stood on the table so the story goes and proceeded to do a Highland Fling lifting up his skirt—sorry, kilt—and showing his tackle! Definitely not a pretty sight from all accounts. Well, that didn't go down well as you can guess. Such behaviour in public, even if it is in front of the depraved, decadent, debauched and dissolute ex-pat English who wouldn't think of calling themselves larger louts (Ah yes, the class system still lives in the UK! That's thanks to your elitist government!), cannot go without comment from our far more refined and easily embarrassed society. Poor Mr Harding had one hell of a time of it from the education bureau and the police but, he did manage to smooth things over. Mind you, Jock Strap, or whatever the teacher's name is, is leaving this summer so the rumours have it. Perhaps he will do his Highland fling elsewhere? On reflection it's probably a good thing that he decided not to do that dance . . . . the Scottish sword dance, I think it's called? . . . . could have been very nasty had he slipped!

Ah, then there was the workers' rebellion. A real show of "enemy at the gates" if you ask me. Again, the school owners had been reluctant to pay the bills (despite the profits they were turning over) and in particular to the workers who had done some renovations etc during the summer vacation. Not enough money to pay the bills but the big boss bought himself a Bentley would you believe? Yes, really! Sometimes, I think some of our comrades have got into the depraved, decadent, debauched and dissolute ways of the British since they seem to mimic them so much. Chairman Mao would never have stood for such behaviour. You can't have a revolution without firing squads I think he said . . . . or was that Lenin? . . . . well, anyway, here is an instance where firing squads would have come in very handy for sure. Bentleys before workers? Reminds me of what was it Hitler said, "Guns before butter"—or was that Goering? Well, that's obviously why they couldn't pay the bills. This is not representative of the new China, trust me. So, one afternoon while the school was happily getting on with its work, outside the main gates the workers congregated. It was a blockade. Come end of school at 3.40 and "they shall not pass." We are not an aggressive

each year they step in and wanted to have a health and safety committee (in China of all places! I ask you?), a say in the school catering so that students got healthy meals daily (in China of all places! I ask you?), more say in the curriculum especially in the area of Mandarin teaching (in China of all places! I ask you?), more say in the PE/Games programme including hair dryers in the swimming pool for students (in China of all places! I ask you?) and I don't know what else. Well, Mr Harding was having none of it. Faced them out he did. Banned the Parents committee and when they objected merely said, "Read my lips!" Powerful stuff. End of fucking story . . . . for quite a while at least. He now has them back on a friends of the school basis so their powers are extremely limited and there will be no more nonsense such as he had before. On reflection, I think Mr Harding would be a great guy for our government! Pity he's not Chinese.

Mad staff, mad workers, mad parents . . . . it's a good job the students aren't mad. Well, no madder than you'd expect 3-18 year olds to be whatever their nationality and wherever they are. Oh, yes, there are some real tearaways but nothing Mr Harding and the staff can't cope with. Anyone out of line and he purges them. Well, that's not the word he uses : he says he expels them. Same difference I suppose.

You're probably wondering how a humble servant like me gets all this inside information. Well, I don't exactly get it from the horse's mouth, so to speak. Sure I sometimes see his purple patches (is that the right phrase?) as we all do but no, I am not party to some of the more behind closed door meetings. However, I am big mates with the best spy in the camp. The guy who may not see it all but certainly hears it talked about and even at times become the confidante of Mr Harding. Yes, you got it! Mr Harding's driver of course. A veritable mine of information and inside knowledge. Stephen, that's his name, is one of my best buddies and we regularly have a great chat over a bottle of scotch (courtesy of mad parents or mad staff or even Mr Harding at times would you believe?) some evenings in my little cubby-hole of an office on site. In vino veritas, as they say.

Well, now. Considering all this aggravation poor Mr Harding gets don't you think he needs some special solace in the arms of a woman out here? Take his mind off things and all that? So, my wife and I hope to engineer this though, as she has already said .... difficult! ....

That's right, dear. Difficult but we hope not impossible ....

BILL

So OK, yeah it's about time I told you how to get by in China. I once thought of giving a title to this bit of my writing—Shanghai Slags and Beijing Broads? Mongolian Molls and China Dolls?. (Not original, I admit!) Nice alliteration on the first three though, don't you think? Could be the title of a musical. Might get round to working on that in my retirement . . . . if I ever retire that is. Well, getting by is not difficult. You just have to get to the right hangouts. Rather than bore you with a list and a run down review of each of them I'll let you into a little secret before I begin. I write poetry! Shock! Horror! Eh? Well, that's not quite true I actually write pastiches based on well known poems, songs etc I am rarely original—I was one of those at school . . . ." good parrots get good marks" type. I find it easy to plagiarise . . . . read into that what you will! Here's a small selection that will definitely help you get by in Shanghai but do heed the warning especially about the Shanghai ladywork crew or girls from the nearby province of Jiangsu from where they may migrate to Shanghai. (I believe—understatement, no I know—similar remarks apply to the Mongolian and Russian girls in Beijing!)

To be sung to the tune of "The Church is One Foundation"

We are all Shanghai ex-pats, a great male company
We find, we feed, we fuck forget many a Shanghai lady
And when our contract's over and homeward we are bound,
We hope at least to get back quite safe . . . . .
. . . . . if not quite sound.

To be sung to the tune of "What friend we have in Jesus"

When this hardship posting's over
No more Long Bar Nights for Me
No more Premiership live action—
And I ain't talkin' TV—
No more 80's nights at Judy's
No more strolls down Hengshan Lu
No sweet girls saying, "Huan Ying Guang Ling"
To miss that jazz makes me feel blue!

"La Belle Dame Shanghaise Sans Merci"
(with apologies to John Keats)

Oh what can ail thee, new ex-pat

Alone and palely loitering?
Have you not heard of Hengshan Lu
And Maoming?

I met a girl in Julu Lu
Who said to me the sweetest thing :
"I will show you Shanghai and teach
You Mandarin."

She led me to The Big Bamboo
To Judy's Too and Fa Fa Bar
And on to Face, Woodstock, BonBon
And to Maya.

Shanghai night life? I saw the lot
But on she led during the day
To Huai Hai and Nanjing Xi Lu
And Xu Jia Hui.

Sight-seeing in Shanghai like this
I found absorbed my whole cash flow
And yet it was that Mandarin
I did not know.

I asked her then about lessons
But she observed I could not pay
So thanked me for such a good time
And went her way!

That's why I sojourn in Shanghai
Alone and palely loitering—
You see I've heard of Hengshan Lu
And Maoming!

I know, now, some of these references are a bit dated given the rate of progress (demolition—same difference!) in a city like Shanghai. Maoming Lu reinvented itself in Tongren Lu but with the development of the new Kerry Centre that has disappeared as well. Hengshan Lu still exists (not quite with the same format as before!) and the big shopping malls in Nanjing Xi Lu, Xu Jia Hui etc still are going strong . . . . and there's plenty more been added since. Well, China has shopping as its new religion! Ladywork still goes on, of course! Oh, and The Long Bar is now called Curve . . . . and someone told me it's a gay bar. Not checked that out myself I must confess (not sure I ever will!) but the new name certainly suggests a difference, don't you think?

MICHELLE WONG

Where was I? India? Yes . . . . well . . . . not really but, thinking logically or laterally or whatever, but just thinking, having mentioned the sub-continent brings me to . . . .

Yoga! Yes. That's the new money spinner I intend to develop now. Well, I have the premises—night clubs are what they say they are! They are exactly what they say on the tin/label/front door? So they are free during the day. Right? Some simple conversion job on a couple of areas making them adaptable for yoga by day and a different kind of yoga by night will not be a big capex investment.

Oh, a licence you ask? What's that you say—"I'm licensed as a night club, not a yoga centre." Don't make me laugh! C'mon, I have told you about my contacts. I have fucking guanxi in spades! The adjective is appropriate, don't you think?

Then there's staff of course. No problem with that. Foreign hire not a problem . . . . (see guanxi—above!) Well, they're all skint (pardon the pun) in India, Indonesia and the like where they practise this art so minimal, not minimum, wage for the new employees. And, of course, residency permits, work permits, accommodation, flights all deductible off the salary! They don't need loads of cash—they hardly eat, do they? Kind of skeletal, anorexic beings and they seem to actually enjoy it! The big bucks come from the punters and all that clothing they love to attire themselves in when doing their exercises. I don't see the clothing manufacturers here having any problem copying the top quality stuff—you know how our factories work—12 hours a day on the real brands and 12 hours a day on the copies/fakes. There's bound to be some mix ups—fallen off the back of a lorry kind of thing! Meiwente! I certainly won't have any qualms about charging the top quality prices!

You see, yoga's a bit like that step aerobics etc you have in the west. The clubs get plenty of members to start but the turnover is high so you are always having to get the new members about every two years. That's not a problem. It's a cyclic fashion. The young, unattached female market here is especially ripe for such exploitation. Many will take up the yoga challenge but how many will actually stay the whole course or stay for more than say two or three years as members? And talking of courses we can introduce yoga teachers' certificates—room there for plenty more income. Of course, the certificates won't really be worth the paper they're printed on but as long as the punters think they're OK, they're OK! Right? We can even link up with travel agents by providing holidays in India, Thailand or in Bali or wherever for the dedicated ones to get that truly deep and meaningful impression that they really have mastered the art and have studied under a real yogi—well, real in the sense, that he's alive and doing the business. I guess the real, real ones are too unworldly to get into anything that smacks of business and finance.

Then there's the food of course. Eco/Bio, organic friendly stuff of course. Salads i.e. rabbit food I think you'd call it in your language. Oh and the fruit juices—specially and freshly squeezed and all that and/or the still or carbonated Evian or Pellogrini water, the former straight from the tap . . . . but freshly bottled. But again, such feeding and watering comes at a price! A highly inflated one, of course.

Oh and we must do a line of cosmetics. Something like Bodyshop. Again, eco-friendly stuff of course. Costs a fortune but is totally ineffective. Thank goodness for that. You never know what those strange tree oils, seaweed extracts, exotic plant fragrances, root shavings, snake venoms, bird droppings and the like might do. This is a case of doing exactly what it definitely doesn't say on the tin/bottle or whatever! Maybe we ought to go for spa treatment as well? It's possible as we have the wet T shirt showers in the club for our clients in the evenings! (That's very popular by the way—much better than a poolside or beach party, I can tell you.) Again, a bit of modification to the water flow and that shouldn't prove to be a problem.

Anything I've forgotten? Yes, O.K. Magazine subscriptions, books, soft music—ethereal type variations on pan pipes, bamboo flute, er-hu stuff, that sort of thing. Yoga gear—tracksuits, yoga mats etc Soft lighting. Just lower the rheostats! Yes, dead easy as we have all that stuff the disco for the night club which plays all the garage type crap at God knows how many decibels and has all manner of coloured, flashing lights that could seriously damage your health! "Weave a circle round him thrice" type stuff!

We need a name of course . . . . I'll think of something appropriate. Nirvanah? No—that's a pop group, isn't it? Yogi World? God no! Too American and everyone will think of Yogi you know who! Let's think. Eureka! Yoni. Yes, Yoni. That's a good name. What are you laughing at? *Yoni* is a Sanskrit word that means source or origin of life. Yes, I know it has sexual connotations and there's nothing wrong with that. (Is there anything that doesn't have, I ask myself?) Yoga is an origin of life—clearing the mind, dying from the materialistic world into the spiritual one—real life. More abundant life. It brings the living to life! Oops mustn't get too carried away on this religious type theme.

Wait a minute! Hey, think of it : Yoni at Den of Iniquity! Don't tell me you're not smiling. I like it. That's what'll be.

Night club? Yoga Centre and Spa? Just differences in degree, not in kind when you think about it. Wow, I have such brilliant business ideas . . . . and the acumen . . . . and the fucking guanxi to make it all work. Ah, yes, I can see it all coming together. A definite money spinner. Good don't you think? I am sure we can think of a suitable name

But that's what business is all about, isn't it? Diversification. But diversification that's clearly linked to the mainstream business. What's the good of running the Den of Iniquity to attract the beautiful, female young things which act as the glittering prizes for the rich, male old things if we can't ensure a constant stream of those beautiful, female young things? (There'll always be a constant flow of rich, male old things, trust me!) Yoga will help to do just that. Might even give discount memberships to the Yoga Club to the really beautiful, female young things.

Mind you there are some middle aged, old females who consider themselves beautiful—what a fucking joke!—whose membership must not be spurned either. Yoga's not cosmetic surgery but the psychological effect for such clients cannot be underestimated. Not by a long way! My friend, well acquaintance really, Jenny Jing, comes into that category. Mutton dressed as lamb, that one! I bet she will jump at the chance of membership. That will be fun. She spurns to visit me here in the club because she doesn't approve of such places but once it undergoes its daily transformation into a yoga den .... and spa, maybe? .... I am sure she'll walk, nay run, through the portals.

She's a bit of a strange woman. Always dressed up like a hambone even when she's gardening! Divorced, of course and dotes on her daughter. Almost suffocatingly so, I would say. She has tried every which way to get her to Lancing International College like Elisabeth but, of course, she hasn't got dual nationality and she certainly doesn't have the guanxi for that turn of events! She's so pretentious having made some good money in the realty business but she doesn't half flaunt it and now thinks she's a cut above her own kind. That's not really a Chinese trait. While many of us have raised ourselves up especially financially we don't spurn, we don't look down on the great and ordinary citizens of our country. You can take the people out of the Cultural Revolution but not the Cultural Revolution out of the people .... except perhaps for the likes of her .... and she really is the exception.

Well, I know she's an item now with that architect chap she's been with but what she doesn't know is he, like many others of his kind spends some of his time in here. He's got the money to attract the ladies, of course. Were she to know this is one of his haunts—I bet he has others—she'd be horrified, naturally. Guess that would be end of fucking story with regard to their relationship! But then, if she was giving him plenty of what he wants, and by the looks of him he needs, he wouldn't come here, would he? Mind you, can he give her what she really wants and by the look of her she really needs? Yes, she needs a man. A real man . . . . in every sense of the word. Would do her the power of good! Thinking about it, he doesn't really look the type who could manage that so maybe they are well suited to each other in that respect. It takes all sorts, doesn't it?

Well, onwards and upwards. I will now need to market the idea of my yoga centre to the powers that be and we'll be open in no time. Actually, I am sure they will just love it. Currently, as I have told you, their wives keep stuffing themselves at Kuadzi while they are stuffing themselves (well not exactly themselves!) silly in a somewhat different way at Den of iniquity, nudge, nudge, wink, wink, know what I mean? Getting their better halves in to do a bit of serious limb twisting—especially in the hot yoga section—will do them a power of good. Get their figures back to some semblance of litheness and trimness again. Their husbands will see me as doing them a really big favour. After all it's embarrassing enough for them to be seen out in their public roles with an aged, dragon lady of a wife dressed up to the nines but it's even worse being seen out with an aged, fat dragon lady of a wife dressed up to the nines and bursting out at the seams of her latest cocktail dress. That's the spin I'll put on things : more diplomatically of course! Can't fail!

I will also mention it to Jenny. Can't wait to see the look on her face. It will be a double take, that's for sure. A yoga centre at a night club? Once she's grasped the concept, bet she'll be first up for membership. She doesn't keep up with the Joneses—she likes to be the Joneses! Mind you it would be funny—I mean funny ha ha—were she to be walking out of here one day after a serious work out when the yoga centre closes and that new architect chappie of hers to be walking in for a serious work out just as the night club opens. Or vice-versa of course! I wonder if I can engineer that? Shouldn't be too difficult!

Oh dear! I have got a devious and evil mind, haven't I? Well, if I hadn't, would I ever have opened my night clubs? Wicked . . . .!

FU

John or should I say Mr.Harding? Mr Harding to his pupils, some of the parents and some of his staff. John to me!

'Twas an evening in November and a night I well remember . . . .

The bar was quiet for sure. Mr Harding—John to me—came in and plonked himself down at the far end of the bar to watch the match on the big screen. He ordered a beer—he loves Kilkenny—and sat there supping away and munching salted peanuts liberally supplied by the bar to encourage drinking. He seemed totally oblivious to anything else but the big screen. Must be a real fan both Eleanor and I thought watching a game such as this which could have no impact up or down on the overall premiership table. Ah well, he was clearly not interested in us and we lost interest in him.

Well, not quite. The call of nature made me have to pass by where he was siting, the ladies' toilet being at that far end of the bar. Conveniently situated, don't you think?

When I came out to walk back to join Eleanor I flashed a weak smile at him which he seemed to totally ignore, still being transfixed by the game on the big screen.

But then came half-time and the call of nature took him to the men's toilets which meant he had to come past the end of the bar where we were sitting and as he passed on his way I flashed a weak smile at him again. Again he seemed to totally ignore it but on the way back to his seat he stopped beside me, sat down and asked if Eleanor and I wanted a drink. After ordering we got talking and Eleanor, bless her, knew she should adjourn as his object of desire was clearly me . . . . and not the footie any more! Well he knew the score (sorry about the pun) and before I knew it we were in a taxi heading to his place.

It was indeed a night to remember. What a great lover he proved to be. Not shy, not inhibited in any way. It was a long time since I had experienced such real orgasmic satisfaction. Wow! Still remembering it almost gives me an orgasm! Well, I was going to say the rest is history but really it wasn't quite like that. Despite the fact that as I said he definitely knew the score he was, in fact, quite shy in his own way especially when in company. He took my mobile phone number but several days went by and he didn't phone me, so I phoned him. He seemed a bit irritated by my call and made no commitment. I was, to tell the truth, disappointed.

Then came Saturday and The Long Bar was filled with members of the Shanghai Strikers Football Club and many others were there to watch the footie on the big screen. And Mr Harding—John to me—turned up. He seemed quite well in with the lads and although I got a smile of recognition from him I got nothing else. He seemed far more into the male camaraderie and was not wanting any female company. Again, I was disappointed.

But Sunday arrived and he called in the afternoon.

"Would you like to share my bed with me tonight?" he asked.

Would I? Oh, yes please I thought. But in order not to sound too keen just muttered a simple, O.K. So we arranged to have dinner together and then went to his apartment. Another great night. It had been worth waiting for. Things went on like this for a couple of months. We were seeing each other at least once and occasionally twice a week. It was O.K. A steady, reasonably regular income and it was always good to be with him. He was so considerate in every way, a real gentleman and he was exceedingly generous when he was prompted to be! He really looked after me and times with him were both exciting and comfortable sexually and socially . . . . respectively!

Obviously staying all night meant he often left me in bed when he went off to work. I was told to lock the door and leave the key under the mat at the entrance which I duly did on all occasions. He trusted me 100% even in those early days! That meant a lot to me. Then, oops! One day I slept in very late and in came his ayi. I expected this to be a classic embarrassing moment for me and for him (in absentia of course!) However, after the initial red faces, stuttered apologies and pregnant pauses it became clear that I seemed to have solved a problem she and her husband had been debating over for a few months. I won't go into details but maybe you'll hear it from them someday! Who knows? To cut a long story short, Jiang Shulin and her husband, Wu Dabin, have become close friends over the years.

I expected him to get angry when I told him the story of meeting with the ayi. But he didn't. He accepted the situation quite readily and we both laughed at it. Again, that meant a lot to me.

Then came the time he asked for a serious talk. I feared the worst. We went to the Long Bar and had one of their bland, tasteless meals washed down with appropriate beverages before we conversed seriously. It was a Wednesday evening—mid week, very quiet. It was short, to the point, serious talk as it turned out but my worst fears were not realised. Rather the opposite. Well, it became more of a negotiation than a talk after he asked, "Would you like to come and live with me?" My heart missed a few beats but suddenly the hard-woman-bitch of

Eleanor's education (should I say indoctrination) clicked in. "Well . . . ."

This was not to be just a simple living, moving lock, stock and barrel event, but a financial transaction. It had to be right. If I was about to give up my life style with its infinite variety (which, to be absolutely honest, custom had staled somewhat) I had to ensure I was able to get all the income and benefits to which I was accustomed, and, as I have already told you, those could be very substantial : very substantial indeed. Well we (or rather I) did the number crunching and eventually settled the details . . . . and the very next day I moved in.

He had a lovely apartment in Xintiandi, generally regarded then and still a very upmarket area of the city. Perfect. But it needed that woman's touch so in went my wardrobe of clothes and his moved to the spare room. Well I had so much more than he had or would ever have for that matter. And now I was with him I would inevitably accumulate more. This is woman! Then there were my photos to display, my ornaments to set out and we had to have some flowers and plants. Give the place a bit of colour, a bit of atmosphere, liven things up a bit. To say he lived a Spartan life would be a serious understatement—I reckon the Count of Monte Cristo had more in his cell at Chateau D'Ifre than Mr Harding (John to me) had in his apartment. Well, that was all changed and I think he appreciated it.

Life was idyllic. We had occasional differences over food at home (i.e. my Chinese home cooking mainly) so we ended up preparing our separate meals but we always agreed on eating out places—isn't that strange? He didn't mind the mouth and lip furnaces type of food shovelled out by Sechuan restaurants and I never minded the bland offerings of Mexican or Indian eating places. But at home . . . .! East is east and west is west and never the twain shall meet . . . . or should that be meat? Well, occasionally we might taste each other's fare but not go much beyond the taste stage.

Love life? As good as ever, though not as frequent but that honestly did not matter to either of us. We both agreed companionship was what our relation was all about and that was as or even was more important than sex : well almost! But he was still a most considerate and excellent lover.

Life style? Holidays abroad and in China. Concerts—pop and classical from the Rolling Stones to Pavarotti, Kylie Minogue to Lan Lan, Christine Aguellira to Yo Yo Ma or should I say Ma Yo Yo! British Chamber of Commerce Balls, Caledonian Balls, Burns' Nights, American Chamber of Commerce Charity events—these all quite new experiences to me but it was good that he felt comfortable about taking me to these events. This meant a lot to me. He even took me to his school events—International Days, concerts, inter school sports etc—which were superb and to school plays which were also most enjoyable, not that I understood them very well. Major sporting events too—I still have the tickets and photos from the first Grand Prix (Formula 1 to us Chinese) held in Shanghai and I saw Federer (and other tennis stars) play in the Shanghai Masters at the fabulous new tennis centre down in the suburb of Minhang. Well, that was just the beginning—there's plenty more I could tell you but I am sure you can see life went on for me much as usual but in a monogamous fashion which I was truly happy about. Oh, and by the way I gave up smoking! And I took up yoga! A fitter and altogether healthier life style.

So it was we lived . . . .

JENNY JING

Bastards! Bastards! All men are bastards!

PETER

The Olympics did us proud, didn't they? I don't just mean China and Beijing. I mean, me, yes me and my family and come to that, Neuschwanstein proud. Oh yes indeed!

You would think that our home being a replica of what Mad King Ludwig built would have attracted the German delegation, well, hangers-on, that is, wouldn't you? Well, that's what I thought, but no! Not a bit of it! Russians. That's who came and took over our palatial abode. Yes. The Russians!

Now I am not talking the Russian athletes : they all stayed at The Olympic Village of course. Mind you I really wish that Yelena Isembayeva, the pole dancer—Oops! Freudian slip!—pole vaulter had decided to stay here rather than there. Could have given her a high time, that's for sure. No, we had the delegation i.e. the hangers-on. The back up, supporting team so to speak. Well, they weren't really a back up team nor really supporters for that matter. They were politicians, men in suits, who'd got time off and freebies to visit China and see their team.

My father was especially pleased I pulled off this deal. (By the way, sadly he had a stroke just before the Olympics and has not fully recovered so is tended to by a couple of nurses mother and I hired. So sad to see him like he is. I only hope he makes some kind of recovery though the doctors seem to think that's not very likely. Can't think what caused it as he's been so healthy all his life.) I had, of course, tried to get the Australians here having contacts from my university days and, as I said thought the Krauts—isn't that what you call them in the UK?—would have jumped at the chance of staying in Neuschwanstein as it would be a kind of home from home so to speak. However, as things turned out I got the Russians through a contact I made at The Den of Iniquity. A very personable lady called Yana it was whom I met there and she managed to put me in touch with the right people. Mind you, she didn't put me on to them right away! I had to use my magnetic charm to wine and dine and you know what her before she introduced me to Ivan and Igor.

Ivan and Igor? Boy did we have some sessions together! Those Russians can really knock it back. Thought we Chinese could do a good job with the moutai and baijiu and all the gan beis but when they get out their vodka! Well, it's nazdorovje in spades! Talk about tight heads and loose balls! You know it made me reflect that Tolstoi wrote those long, tedious, boring novels to get over his hangovers and to avoid having to go out two or more nights on the spin with the lads. "Oi! You comin' out for a session tonight, Leo?" the lads would have shouted. "Sorry," he would have said, head throbbing like mad and with a throat like the inside of a squash player's glove, "got to catch up on my writing!" "Boring bastard," would have come the reply and he was, wasn't he. Wow, his novels could and did bore for Russia! C'mon, have you read all your way through War and Peace? or Anna Karenina? Well, anyway, they were great sessions with Ivan and Igor and I found them such easy guys to do business with. Who was it wrote, "Let us drink 'til we roll under the table in vomit and oblivion"? Can't remember but that's exactly what we did on more than one occasion, I'm telling you. They also introduced me, would you believe, to the delights of a first course curry meal (Vindaloo, of course!) before hitting the alcohol. Certainly helped to soak up the liquor but, oh my God, those fan tail shits the next morning! Happy days!

Turned out these two lads were attached to The Russian Embassy in Beijing and, among other things had been instrumental in getting Yana a permit to reside in China which was exceedingly nice of them, don't you agree? Good guys, zhen de! So we got talking and had some of those great sessions round my place. It knocked them out. No, not the drinking sessions (though they did, of course)—Neuschwanstein, naturally! What else? They realised our fairy tale castle had all the space they needed for the Russian delegation who, they said, had been desperately searching for the right venue in Beijing so they could come over and support their team. The rooms and general space they indicated were not a problem—plenty of both—but we had to put in some amenities to make it a real goer for this clientele.

So it was we did some additions to our site and to the decoration of the interior. Would you believe we added a massive ice rink? Yes, indeed. Not too difficult really, just a hole in the ground, though a pretty big one admittedly with frozen surface water and no, we didn't make it a permanent structure but had it covered by a big marquee. Cost a bit mind you and the upkeep of it in Summer when they were here proved a tad more expensive than I would have liked but when you want to attract the right sort of customers you've got to invest accordingly.

Then we had to make up a mini theatre—well, not so much mini as maxi—for their floor shows, keep them interested and entertained (should I say occupied?) in the evenings. That was a reasonable request and it was not that big a renovation job. Although well situated near the motorways to the city, we are a bit far out. Not isolated exactly but definitely on the outskirts of our lovely city. We had the space so it was no great trouble but the lighting and sound system again were a bit pricey but when you want to attract the right sort of customers you've got to invest accordingly.

The other bits were easy. Get rid of some of the wines in our cellars. To be honest they weren't exactly vintage except in the sense that they were old having been lying there for ages. Replaced with vodka : what else? Ivan and Igor were really helpful on this score. They not only took away most of the wine, free, gratis and for nothing but they got a great discount in the importing fee for all the vodka we had to bring in. I could hardly believe it. Amazing what a cash payment rather than waiting for an invoice, sending a cheque and getting a receipt can do, isn't it? I was very happy that they managed to take this matter into their own hands so I had no qualms about handing over the money without batting an eyelid.

Finally we hired some Russian musicians and Cossack dancers, again friends of Yana's, Ivan's and Igor's, so they too came at a very reasonable price. This troupe was around during the time the delegation were visiting and with their music and dancing gave the place a bit of a home from home atmosphere for them. Just to add to that we hung up some extra chandeliers, got in various items such as samovars, stuck up some posters of Lenin, Marx, Engels, Stalin, Breshnev, Kruschev, Putin et al and draped a few hammer and sickle flags here and there, changed the menu to include among other things borsch, caviar, beef stroganoff and suddenly Neuschwanstein takes on the image of the Winter Palace or some such! Long live the proletarian revolution!

Well, when all the guys turned up, yes it was all men interestingly enough, they absolutely loved it. Yana said we should offer a variety of entertainment in the theatre so she got a lot of friends, mainly Mongolian females interestingly enough, to come and perform along with the dancers and musicians in the evenings at our mini, or rather, maxi theatre. They went down a storm as you can well imagine. I sometimes think the Russians enjoyed what happened here in the evening more than they enjoyed the Olympics. Their team didn't exactly cover themselves with glory, did they? Only just pipped the UK in the medals table by the end of it all. It was a great two and a half weeks and I was able to see a lot of Yana in that time though, to be honest, she was kept quite busy and yes, I saw her, but on most occasions that's indeed all I did.

It was all over too soon. The delegation didn't stay for the disabled games since they said they had too much on in Moscow and St Petersburg. Ivan and Igor turned up to see them all off and we celebrated that evening toasting the Chinese naturally since they had topped the medal table on their home soil.

It seems a bit of a faded memory now and all we have left is this hole in the ground (must get it filled in when we can afford it) outside where the ice rink was, some extra chandeliers which, when I see them sparkling when we can afford the electricity to switch on their lights remind me of Yana and her deep, sparkling black eyes, a heap of Russian utensils, posters and flags and a theatre which is gathering dust. Not much to show for that happy fortnight and a bit! Strangely the ice rink didn't get that much use except for the occasional brawling ice hockey games, if you can call them games! They were mainly ad hoc events when the delegates had imbibed a little too much of the vodka.

Ivan and Igor have left the embassy here I have heard. Tried phoning them after our post Olympics drinking session but was politely told they weren't there any more. I guess they got promotion back to Moscow after the great work they had done here for their comrades. Maybe if I go to Moscow sometime I will try to look them up.

Yana. Ahhhhh, Yana? Sparkling, black-eyes, beautifully bosomed, leggy Yana! Well, I see her occasionally but only on her occasional visits and these are indeed very occasional so all I get to do is see her when she comes to Beijing. She's working in Shanghai now in social services there. I don't travel to Shanghai that often, hardly ever in fact, well never to be precise, so we see each other, yes, that's all we do, see each other when she's up here recruiting. Happy memories though. Can't beat the memories she gave me.

Father, as I said has not fully recovered and it's doubtful if he ever will. He missed out on the Olympics really and, of course, all the fun at home though we did take him in his wheel chair to see the ladies beach volley ball. I think from the smiles on his face—he cannot talk as a result of the stroke—he enjoyed that as did the whole Russian delegation who came along to that event. Mother had a great time. She really enjoyed the company of the delegates, lapped it up and indeed got lots of invites to go to Moscow which I know she would love to take up but she feels a bit unhappy about leaving father in his current state. I try to encourage her to make the effort and even now, sometime after the event I hope she will manage to go.

Me? Well I got a bit of stick from my wife and kids in Bangkok for not inviting them and getting them and their extended family tickets and bringing them all over but as I explained, this was a business venture for me and it would have been difficult to have them here with me when I was wheeling and dealing! I pocketed a tidy sum from the event courtesy of Ivan and Igor but some of the costs left a sizeable dent in the management account for our abode. But, what the hell? Get into another business venture and recoup the losses : that's my motto. Nothing springs immediately to mind but Yana suggested the musicians and dancers together with the Mongolian girls could have

WU DABIN &
JIANG SHULIN

I vividly remember the morning I went to Mr Harding's apartment and there was this lady (sic) in his bed. Well, you could have knocked me down with a feather! Truly flabbergasted I was. She was surprised and I was astonished. As you will have gathered, I am not a prude but it seemed so out of character for Mr Harding. He had his wife and some members of his family staying with him before and sometimes some friends just for the odd weekend or week and he'd always told me about those in advance of course. They say still waters run deep and that certainly applies to Mr Harding. But this indeed left me, how do you say—gob smacked? Like your footballer who came and played in China : Paul Gascoigne or Gazza as you called him. When he was booked in that world cup semi-final so many years ago he started blubbering like a baby. Strange behaviour and strange name or should I say nickname that. He wasn't as good as Stevie Gerrada or David Beckhamo. Moreover he spoke a very strange version of English—at least that's what they reported in the papers here. Well, Gascoigne is a French type family name isn't it so I guess he was speaking Franglais or something like that. Yes indeed, I was absolutely, truly gob smacked at least initially.

At first I was not sure how to react and neither was the young lady (sic). So initially we just exchanged pleasantries and I decided to get on with my job while she got on with getting dressed. She was obviously intent on leaving as soon as possible but it was apparent she was upset that Mr Harding would be angry with her so she wanted to confide in me before she left. She was very concerned. Should she tell him? What should she tell him? How might he react. Was I upset or angry about the situation? There was a deal of anxiety in her voice and she was close to tears at times. Clearly she was embarrassed—we both were—but it was clear she cared for Mr Harding and didn't want him to lose face or be shamed by her tardiness. I could feel that emotional side to her character and I liked it. I empathized with it.

So we had a chat. There and then. A chat. A very English chat over a cup of very Chinese, pu er tea . . . . but without the cream cakes! I liked her and I think, no I knew, she liked me. We seemed to hit it off without much difficulty. I told her that I felt the sensible thing to do was for her to admit to Mr Harding what had happened. I could see no harm in that for although I knew he could get worked up into one of his purple patches (to use my better half's phrase) at work, making intractable problems inherent from his bosses and parents' problems tractable, he had infinite patience with those whom he liked or for those for whom he had respect and I am sure Ms Fu—Fu as she became known to me—definitely fell into one of those categories. This seemed to set her mind a bit more at ease though I think she still left with a tinge of doubt about my advice. However, my counsel proved to be right as when I went to the apartment subsequently and almost ever since she had become the Lady of The Manor so to speak. Not, mark you, in the condescending, high falootin' manner, laying down the law to plebs like me but having control as to what happens in the apartment. She started to give the place that feminine touch—pictures, plants, throw-overs, photos, ornaments and what not : you know the sort of thing. And boy did the place need that! Mr Harding's Spartan regime prior to Fu's incumbency is a good example of litotes.

She is a great girl. Zhen de! She made my work easy as she was always ready to muck in with the cleaning, laundry and whatever and that gave us both time to have more English chats over quite a few more cups of Chinese, pu er tea. And, since she had some control over the purse strings, we could add cream cakes now! She was lonely, I think—well, not lonely in the evenings and night times or weekends as she had Mr Harding as her companion to keep her warm . . . . and I am sure he was good at doing that . . . . but during the day when there was not much for her to do.

Well for me and Mr Wu it was problem solved. Englishman had got his Chinese wife. He was evidently happy and we were happy for him. And they really made a nice couple. We enjoyed quite a few evenings out together thanks to Mr Harding's generosity. He's not the type of ex patriate who's always up his own arse! Certainly not the No Dogs, No Chinese type. He was always fun to be with; we did not understand anything he said and he did not understand anything we said. We would simply smile and nod at each other in absolute lack of comprehension and a kind of incredulity. Fu helped him and us from time to time with translations. How accurate they were I really cannot say. Does it really matter? I most assuredly think not. Happy days!

And they were made even happier with my daughter's wonderful experience in England at the Summer language school course she attended, kindly funded by Mr Harding. She came back bright-eyed and bushy tailed and a lot more proficient in English . . . . I think. Well, Mr Wu and I hope so for as aforesaid, we don't speak the lingo. Having said that Mr Wu has now a good knowledge of English that applies to his work and a little more besides from what I gather. However, cisterns, ducts, waste pipes, circuit breakers, 4 x 4 adapters, putty, plugs, screws, bolts, bulbs, manhole covers, plumb lines, radiators, air-conditioners, sockets and what have you don't exactly make for scintillating conversation topics and won't be much use to my daughter . . . . though they might, in time be, to my son!

Anyway, she brought back some lovely presents for us all : fridge magnets depicting your famous Winston Churchill, your Queen—what a lovely woman—and the Beatles which she referred to as the Fab Four but they honestly don't mean much to us. She also brought a tea pot in the Shape of The Houses of Parliament and a tin of Earl Grey (but what we would really call Earl Black) tea. For my son, Gary, she brought a couple of T shirts, one with Cambridge University on it (fat chance of his getting to that educational establishment!) and one with the underground map of London. That would be worth wearing in case you got lost in the city I guess. She also brought some strange sweets called Edinburgh rock which she said was named after the capital city of Scotland and it did have the picture of a nice castle on the box as well as some tartan stripes. Why it was called rock (*yanshi* in our language so out daughter told us) we couldn't work out? Really too soft and sugary to be called by such a name. But the McVities shortbread biscuits (which, in fact you can get in the City Supermarket and elsewhere here!) were nice and she would have got them duty free! Plenty of cigarettes and whisky as well and that really made her Dad's, and her uncles' and her cousins' little angel. Of course she had loads of photographs from her trip and we and our relatives and friends spent lots of time flicking through them and poor girl she had to give us a commentary on each one. With all these family gatherings we soon got through the cigarettes, whisky, the shortbread biscuits and even the Edinburgh rock. Waste not, want not!

We had fun listening to the names of those Cambridge Colleges. Jesus. Jesus? What do you Christians make of that? Christ's. Christ's? What does your Christian church make of that? King's? Queen's? Sounds like a game of chess. Or is it a reflection on the gay community at the university? Then just a list of peoples' names—Clare, Selwyn, Fitwilliam, Robinson, Downing, Churchill : but who the hell was Corpus Christi? Well none of it really made sense to us but we did find it funny enough. We never use names like that. It would be an insult to have somewhere named Mao Zedong University, Zhou En Lai College, Deng Xiao Ping Academy or Jiang Zemin School or whatever. However, we are happy to have those guys and others displayed on T shirts now, on playing cards and on fridge magnets and even cushions and umbrellas so perhaps we are starting to adopt some of your western ways and who knows? Maybe those university and college names are no so far off?

Then there was London. She had photos of her outside The Houses of Parliament, The Tower of London, on The London Eye, on the River Thames (in a boat of course, not literally on it as she can't do the walking on water trick . . . . yet!) outside Buckingham Palace, near number 10 Downing Street where your Prime Minister lives next to someone whose job is Chancellor of the Exchequer, whatever kind of job that is! Evidently you can't go down Downing Street because of terrorists : no, I don't mean because there are terrorists there but I mean it's protected against terrorists going down there. Then she was in Trafalgar Square surrounded by pigeons. Everyone was feeding the pigeons—all a bit strange, shouldn't the pigeons be feeding us? Down the road she said was where she was photographed beside some guys strangely dressed in old uniforms and on horseback and carrying swords. These were guards so she told us. Guards? With swords? On horseback? When was the last cavalry charge by English troops? In India in the 19th century perhaps. These guys looked good but I wouldn't give them much chance against someone with a Kalashnikov. Moving on there she was proudly standing in front of the Globe Theatre. Strange you should build an actual building to make it look old and genuine : and you criticize us for fakes and breaking intellectual property rights! Of course she went on down Oxford Street where she said she felt quite at home because of the McDonalds, Starbucks, Costa Coffees, Kentucky Fried Chicken, Pizza Huts, Marks and Spencer, H & M, Zara and the big department stores with Gucci, Ferragamo etc. Finally she made it to China town where she said she could get some real Chinese food .... well almost real but certainly not the wide variety of food we get out here. Of course, going there didn't help her English as she was able to natter away in Chinese to heart's content to the workers there. Well, I guess this together with Oxford Street added to her comfort zone and we all need a bit of security, familiarity when we are tourists or strangers in a strange land.

She obviously had a great time and made lots of new friends. There was she said one other Chinese girl on her course. Lala was her name. "One of the Tele Tubbies," giggled Dong Dong when she mentioned the name. "Who the hell are the Tele Tubbies?" I asked myself. Lala was from Beijing. They got on great so she said. They correspond now mainly by skype, email and text messages of course. Guess it won't be long until they decide to visit each other. Very nouveau jeunnesse. She also keeps in touch with some of her other friends around the globe and has even got what she calls a proxy server so she can contact them via her laptop on Face Book which is banned here. All too hi tec for me. I guess it's all good for her English practice.

We are ever so grateful for Mr Harding for subbing this trip for our lovely daughter. She has something to remember for the rest of her life and so have we. It was even like being there with her looking at those photos and when we look at our gifts like the fridge magnets, or when Gary wears one of his T shirts, or we use the tea pot or we remember drinking the whisky, eating the Edinburgh rock, the shortbread and smoking the cigarettes it well, it could have been us on that trip. Virtual travelling I guess you'd call it. A bit more realistic than what you get on your VDUs. Finally I forgot to tell you she brought us a cookery book with recipes for UK meals like roast beef, prawn cocktail, cod and chips, toad in the hole, apple pie and ice cream—well, that's what she told us was in it because we can't read it of course. Must be honest, the pictures of the dishes don't look all that inviting so Mr Wu, Gary and I decided we will stick to drunken prawns, beggar's chicken. dan dan mian, Ducks' tongues, pigs' intestines, deep fried insects, hairy crab and the like. Yummy!

MICHELLE WONG

And so it came to pass : I opened Yoni! Should I rephrase that? No, I don't think so. Another instant and resounding success. What can I say? Was I right or was I right? No, the jury's definitely not still out on that! It's made up its mind—success equals good business, equals profit, equals money and lots of it. Loadsamoney! Ah, don't you just love it when a plan comes together? I certainly do. Oh, c'mon, we all do. Sure we do.

Well onwards and upwards.

Oh, before I go on, yes the cunning, conniving conspirator in me dropped Jenny Jing right in it. Serves her right—it couldn't happen to a nicer person! What's that? There's horns growing out of my head and a forked tail out of my arse. There she was, dressed up like a hambone as usual, happily trotting in for her early, dare I say well needed, yoga session and there was architect boyfriend on his way out, somewhat hung over and somewhat still hammered and therefore being helped out by two gorgeous, scantily attired young ladies. The look of horror on her face would have got her a lead role in Hammer Films. She stopped in her tracks and cried out in a high pitched scream, "Well I never!" (in Chinese of course!) To this he sluringly with an inane grin on his face replied, "Well, I did! More's the pity for you!" End of love's young (sic?) dream, big time! End of fucking story. (Did it ever start? Think!) Ah, don't you just love it when a plan comes together? I certainly do. Oh. C'mon, we all do. Sure we do.

Of course the world does not stand still while all these things are going on. Peter has been in to The Den of Iniquity a lot recently living of what he claims are his takings *From Russia with Love* Olympics success. Well it's his latest story and puts the American education saga on the back burner thank God. But everyone, even the dumb blondes here (well we do have some Russian ladies among our Den of Iniquity clientele) can see how he was conned. He's the only one still in the dark. Maybe it's better that way. Ignorance is bliss after all. Sadly his father was taken ill by it all and is now confined to a wheel chair and it has been reported he will be unlikely to recover. Not so much the sins of the father being visited downwards but the sins of the son being visited upwards; the Bible got things back to front. Well, that's the story of that book, isn't it? Who had the really good times? Was it Ruth—"Whither thou goest" and all that. Boring! Or was it the likes of Jezebel and Delilah? They may have come to an unhappy end but they had a great time getting there. O.K. So Bunyan's Christian, the eponymous Pilgrim of his novel, eventually got to the Delectable Mountains and beyond but he had one hell of a time getting there, didn't he? Would you want to go through all that—Slough of Despond, Doubting Castle and Giant Despair, Vanity Fair etc. You pays your money and you takes your choice.

Whilst it's good to sit back and see it all happening on the nightclub front, the yoga front and my initial restaurant front it's important to think ahead. So where do I go from here? Well, the purpose of any business is to make a profit and the bigger the profit the better. In that respect the restaurant whilst doing good business is the least profitable of my enterprises so I am considering selling it off. There's plenty of buyers around : there's a Thai group of restaurants that wants to diversify so Kuadzi would be good for them. They have approached me already and seem willing to offer a good price. But what do I do with that and all the money I am earning elsewhere? I must be careful. Yes, I've made a packet as you would say but I keep well clear of the 100 richest Chinese list—we call that the Death List and I am sure you can work out why! I've heard Mongolia is opening up. Lots of mineral resources and therefore a lot of interested mining companies, especially from Australia. Now, we all know a Chinese with Aussie connections, don't we? Yes, Peter will come in useful or I shall convince him he can do so. So watch this space . . . .

In the interim I will spend time with my family. Well, with my daughter at least. Husband is in Hong Kong. We've kind of separated I suppose you'd say. At least in distance terms for the time being. Who knows about the future? Elizabeth is with me and is doing well at Lancing where she takes her IGCSEs this year. I want her to do her sixth form (I prefer the traditional nomenclature to the Years 12 and 13) in the UK. Kind of finishing school approach but I believe if she goes there she will be with a more mature group of students and she will have a better chance to suss out and then get a good place at one of the universities there. She'll be on the doorstep after all. So I am researching options and to date I am pretty appalled by some of the things I have found on school web sites. I mean, for instance, get this from a web site I recently looked at : and this is from a pukka independent school, believe me. It reads :-

One of school X's distinctive contributions in education is to be developing classes in well-being (colloquially called 'happiness classes')in association with Oxbridge University's Institute for Well-Being. This approach is aimed at developing intra personal intelligence. These classes will help pupils learn how to look after their minds, bodies and emotional intelligence better, how to develop relationships and pursuits which will aid them through life, and how to identify their priorities and to fulfil their own goals and aspirations for their lives. The curriculum, extra curricular and pastoral life of school X will all be designed specifically to promote an all round approach to education in its widest sense. When pupils leave at 18 they will be presented at a special graduation ceremony with the School X Certificate of Achievement which will specify each child's achievements in all fields of life at school X.

Bloody hell, I hope it's me who can give my daughter happiness classes and that they are not taught—can they be taught?—by some third hand public school teacher who wears a corduroy jacket with leather patches on the elbows and rims on the cuffs and whose skimpy beard is as virginal as they come. Like the Bible I reckon it could be the other way round. My daughter would just say, "get a life" to such a geek. All fields of life at the school? What a fucking joke! When they leave at 18 they will get a Certificate of Achievement? What in for fuck's sake? Happiness? Intra personal intelligence? Emotional intelligence? Whatever those last two are or mean. I don't want my daughter to get that kind of certificate. I can give her that kind of certificate. That's not what she needs. What am I going to be paying outrageous fees for? I want her to get passes in exams. Certificates in exam passes in the subjects she has studied, not in 'achievement.' That's what's going to get her to university not a certificate that's not worth the vellum (yes, I guess they print it on that and that what the fees are paid for) it is delicately, italically scrolled (by the Art teacher no doubt—helps their profits) upon!

Sadly, that quote and that sort of thing it's going on about are typical of many others. No wonder the UK is going to the dogs. By the way when you go there do you see everybody happy? All singing and dancing in the street? Place you really want to be? Personally, and I have travelled a lot, I fell a considerable amount of disaffection from everybody when I am there. The weather doesn't help of course : too much drizzle, fog and damp. Not enough rays of sunshine. Certainly not conducive to happiness. Many faces look beefy, grubby and grey just like the meat in that standard dish of shepherd's pie. Maybe they do need happiness so I should transport my Yoni and Den of Iniquity there. Have you ever ready such namby mamby crap? Maybe I ought to put her into a sixth form in a Chinese school. 40 plus in a class. Front of classroom delivery, lecture style. Students get their heads down, make notes, swot up (6 hours homework every night!) and take and, what's more, pass exams. With top quality passes not the Ds and Es of watered down A Levels. Squat toilets. Minimal décor throughout the classroom and corridors. Long school days. Really knackers them. Sends them home tired but educated. We'll do the happiness bit (or otherwise) at home thank you very much.

Really sorry to go on but I feel like I am plagiarizing Dylan Thomas in his remark about the Welsh National Anthem . . . . Land of my Fathers . . . . and they're welcome to it! Well, Britain, my Britain. Land of my and my daughter's passport and that's about all it's good for. And it really is, isn't it? Civis Brittanus Sum. Useful and well worth the money! No. I am exaggerating. I don't mean to be so disparaging of dear old Blighty but reading such claptrap gets my goat. But I am certainly going to send her to a UK school and I have plenty of friends there (and here) who will give me the best advice—or at least they'd better or bang goes their membership of the Den of Iniquity. I am sure she'll do OK and I look forward to her getting a place at Uni over there. That will make me, (Oh! and her father of course!) very proud.

Oh, hang on a minute. Message on my mobile.

Oh, would you believe? Jenny Jing! Needs a shoulder to cry, or should I say, keep crying on. Poor dear. She needs some happiness in her life. Yes, I can do happiness. She's so naïve about men, about women, about life! And yet she's intelligent; but there's no direct correlation between intelligence and street savvy is there? Now there's something you can't teach : street savvy. Should I diversify into education and try to run such classes? There's a thought. Should I recommend she reads The Art of War or The Prince? Even were I to do so she would read them clinically and critically and fail to extract their base line meaning. Better that she reads A Concise Chinese—English dictionary for Lovers by Xiaolu Guo—offers far more insights into the love world of Chinese women at home and abroad. She's a sad case and regrettably, no I really mean that, I have made it sadder. Time to make amends. Time to change tack and cheer her up. Wish me luck. I need to right a wrong.

JENNY JING

Please excuse my last outburst. So very unlike me, I do assure you. However, circumstances and all that. I won't go into details. Just too dreadful as far as I am concerned but I am sure you can surmise what has happened. Leave it to your imaginations. Still, life goes on. I guess I'll have to wash that man right outta my hair as the song says. I have my own life and that of my daughter's to think about. Can't dwell on that. The worst place to live is in the past.

Michelle came over to see me. Bless her! Well, actually, I did text her about things. Got to have someone to confide in when such things happen. She was ever so kind and sweet. Brought me some beautiful Belgian chocolates and a wonderful bouquet of flowers and, more importantly as far as I was concerned, gave me a lot of TLC and most welcome it was. I really appreciated that. A true friend in need and all that!

Actually she spiced up all the talk with an idea about a new business venture. She has her eyes on Mongolia which is opening up because of all its mineral wealth. Quite rightly she said a lot of Australian companies were involved and she was going to contact Peter Zhang about his old school contacts in that country and see if there were any suitable avenues worth pursuing. She suggested to me that there would be real estate opportunities if all goes well and I must say I absolutely agree with her on that. Well, we both agreed to see what Peter can produce and we know we can sweet talk him into getting involved and even investing and thereby making more money for us . . . . while promising him he well be kept more than flush for his visits to the Den of Iniquity. As Michelle said, we can always entice him with Mongolian women and she has plenty of those who frequent her clubs. Well, he has got a one track mind! This is Man! They keep their brains between their legs, don't they? Oops did I really say that? Actually I'm quoting Michelle! Sure enough, this proposed venture has given me a focus and hopefully a new opportunity in the future and that will take my mind off things and help me get over recent events. When one door closes as they say.

Talking of which my daughter came back quite perked up from her UK adventure. Yes she really enjoyed the UK and yes, her English had most certainly improved. Must say I will definitely recommend the Camera School of English in Cambridge. Seems to have worked wonders for her and she's a lot less shy now than she was before she went away. Much more grown up so I know I did the right thing by sending her there on her own and not, as my original intention was, to chaperone her trip. Wonderful to see. It has been really good chatting with her about all the places she had visited and looking at her photos .... Cambridge, Oxford, London, Bath, Stratford Upon Avon etc. A great experience for her. She brought me back a book, *How to speak Scouse* : a really nice, thoughtful present! So sweet of her. That really took me back to my days in Liverpool when I studied there. Maybe if I'd had that in those days I would have socialized more with the locals, or at least understood what they were saying at times. Ah, fond memories. But mustn't get maudlin. The worst place to live is in the past!

Of course, she'd made a lot of friends. Even one based in Shanghai who was on the course with her. A young lady called Dong Dong about the same age as her so she tells me. Daughter of an international school maintenance manager and whose mother works as an ayi is what she says. Where they got the money to afford such a course for their daughter I don't know! Hmmmm. A bit suspicious that! Well, it seems they both got on well and I guess it's good to have some familiar company from one's own country when being a stranger in a strange land. They correspond on email and by text and skype of course. Par for the course with the youth of today! However, I won't let her use Facebook. Yes, I know it's possible to get on to it even though it is technically banned here but I agree with my government's policy on this : social networking via such a system can be dangerous and can lead to problems. I have heard of some families having major rifts with their youngsters because of this. So that's definitely off limits! She does plead with me at times, but on this subject I am adamant. Well, no doubt she'll be wanting to go on a visit to Shanghai soon or will be asking me if Dong Dong can come and stay here for a few days soon. Fair enough. It will provide her with some company, hopefully stop her pleading about Facebook and come to that will probably make the house a bit more cheerful in these somewhat, depressing personal times.

Oops, sorry, mustn't get down in the dumps.

Well, there's certainly a known cure from a women's point of view for how I feel. Shopping! In China we used to have Taoism, Buddhism, Confucianism, Christianity, Marxism, Mao Zedong Thought and whatever but now we have replaced all these. So it is that our spiritual void is now replaced with shopping. The new Chinese religion. *Die einkaufen is das opium des volkes*—well, that's what I think Marx ought to have written or perhaps he would write were he alive today. It's not just a women's thing here to be honest. Our cities have become one or should I say several great shopping malls! So now I think I'll blow a few (well more than a few actually!) renminbi down at Sanlitun North Village. It's not been open long. They built the Sanlitun South Village for the Olympics and there's loads of sports shops there : Adidas, Nike, Puma and what have you. And, of course, the big Beijing Apple store is situated there. But they have taken a bit of time finishing off the north part but all the really great shops, restaurants etc are there : Balenciaga, Gucci, Versace, Balmain, Ferragamo, Hermes, Alexander McQueen, Let's Burger! Yes will get out and about and splash the cash as they say. Maybe go OTT a bit in anticipation of the Mongolian mineral rush! It's about time I treated myself to a new outfit, new accessories, new shoes, new jewelry and as Michelle said maybe even a new man . . . . and a better man to boot! Are there any around I wonder? Doubt it but I guess I will have to live in hope.

Life really is a roller coaster is it not? That sounds familiar, certainly not original. Maybe I heard it on one of Oprah's shows. Or did Michelle give me that quote as well?

FU

I was going to say happily ever after but I can't. Oh, I so dearly wish I could. Truly I do. But reality and honesty won't let me. So how did it all end? Well, not end exactly, for it's not ended as you will learn, but change, for change it certainly did.

Was it money? O.K. There were some occasional arguments over that but who doesn't argue about money? It's not money that is the root of all evil but lack of it I think by the way. I readily admit I was a bit demanding at times but I was also critical of him dishing out money to his family who were certainly old and independent enough and should have been looking after themselves. A bit hypocritical of me I must confess. But in my view that's the opposite of our culture : the young look after the old, not vice versa as he was doing. I felt he was being taken advantage of. Pot calling the kettle black? You're entitled to your opinion. However, I soon learned to tread very carefully in that respect. Family, he always said, was most important to him. Yes, he would say, you can choose your friends but not your family but he chose his family and that was that. Subject off limits!

Was it sex? Oh no! Definitely not! Though we may not have indulged as newly weds or teenagers after their first taste of the forbidden fruit, we certainly indulged and that was never a problem. Our sex life was very, very good. Oh, and he didn't need Viagra by the way, despite our age difference. He used to use an odd expression saying he had "throbbings of noontide"—a phrase he explained to me from one of his favourite writers who was writing about getting old. But Mr Harding—John to me—was hardly getting old! In my opinion he was better off using Elton John's phrase . . . I'm still standing!" But not with Elton John proclivities of course!

Was it another woman? Or women? Well, again the answer's no. Oh, I have my suspicions that on the occasions I went home to see my family he may well have found a temporary solution to fill the gap left by my absence. Or should I say he found a temporary gap to fill as a solution left by my absence? But if he did, it was never serious and what the eye doesn't see and all that. And anyway, it wasn't out of sight out of mind as he always gave me the impression that absence had made his heart (or if not his heart another key part of his anatomy) grow (a most appropriate verb for sure!) stronger.

So, what was it caused the change?

Work, that's what! Can you believe that? Yes, work came between us. Or rather the distance of just over 1,700kms caused by work. Yes, that's right. He had to move to Beijing. To the capital in the frozen north from the humid (and damp) south! From the financial to the political PRC world. There's no point in going into the details. These things happen with expatriates. They are not always masters of their own destinies and I mean that in every sense of the phrase especially since they are working in China!

At first he said he would take me with him and I was overjoyed by that. But then he changed his mind. Came up with all sorts of reasons. He needed his own space. Wasn't sure how long the Beijing transfer would last : it was, after all, just a new educational project for the company he'd opened the international school for. Might be all over very quickly. Felt he would be taking me further away from my family. Separation had to happen sometime. We both ought to get used to it. Wanted to see how things went in Beijing before committing himself there and asking me to join him. Sounds plausible enough, does it not?

At first I was devastated of course. Cried me a river (almost literally!) and sobbed my heart out. (But didn't end up blind or dead!) Inconsolable I was. I couldn't be angry with him. He had treated me so, so well and in some ways I could understand his reasons to a certain extent. But I felt my world, my whole future was about to collapse. But what could I do? I had no right to force him into taking me with him. O.K. I was well set up financially : I had my apartments and my friends in my home town and I had no worries about having a roof over my head and economic survival but I needed him. Yes, honestly I needed him. He had become an anchor in my life and I was not prepared to let him go. I know that sounds selfish and to a degree it was but we all want safety and security in life and that's exactly what he had given me. And who is it won't fight for something they really want?

As it was when we talked about the situation I could see, no rather I could feel, or more certainly I knew he was trying to convince himself of the need for our separation as much as he was trying to convince me. I could see, no rather I could feel, or more certainly I knew he was as sad and downcast about the state of affairs as I was. However, it was as if he was going to be masochistic about it towards himself and therefore sadistic about it towards me. (What was it the sadist said to the masochist who had asked him to flog him? No, of course!)

I decided to cut out the tears and they weren't the usual waterworks, crocodile ones of our sex—these were the real thing, trust me. I wanted to prove to him I was a big girl (well, I'd already done that in many ways) but I guess I wanted just to show him I was going to be strong,

I was mature and could deal with the situation although I should have said to him, Ni bu dong wode xin! But maybe he did understand my heart after all.

I certainly understood his heart. It turned out he was the kind of guy who just can't say no. Well, at least not a direct no. He has to qualify it. He hates to have to let people down. He's the kind of guy who would answer, "Well, yes and no," were he asked if he had trouble making decisions. Decisions in terms of human relationships that is. He's like the schizophrenic who sees a lecture on schizophrenia but is in two minds as to whether or not to attend! However, I know from Mr Wu, and others I might add, that he could be almost dictatorial in his professional life and never has trouble making up his mind on matters related to his work. He even wrote an article on decision making for an educational publication. "Get the Facts; Weigh and Decide; Take Action; Check results." Those were his guide lines. But when having to decide in matters of personal relationships, the social network as it's referred to, he was all at sea. Despite his clinical, theoretical approach he knew when it comes to the crunch with people the heart has its reasons as you would say. Trouble is, he cared about people too much, especially people he liked and, dare I say, loved. That, in my opinion, was the trouble with his family relationships but let's not go down that road. Tread carefully!

So we got a tolerable compromise. We would in fact be separated at least geographically. He would pay for a small apartment for me so I could stay in Shanghai and not have to go home to my boring home town with its Buddhist Monastery and where people lived ordinarily ever after. He would get set up in Beijing and I could visit him whenever I wanted and he would pay my travel costs. Not a bad deal eh? Oh, and he also gave me a generous living allowance by direct transfer to my bank so I could continue to be a lady of leisure. Well, that's how I term myself. You may think otherwise. That's your prerogative. Quite honestly I don't give a flying fuck what you think! Oops, sorry! Didn't really mean that! Just slipped out as the archbishop said to the actress.

So we entered a new phase of our relationship. And, although initially there were teething problems, it grew to be a pretty good way of life for both of us.

I had friends in Shanghai so I was relatively happy in many ways about not having to leave there though I did miss him especially at weekends when we used to have such fun together in what is after all a great, vibrant city! I missed going out to the nice restaurants for brunches and dinners : I missed the deafening sounds of the Fillipino Band in Malone's especially when they were playing Sweet Child of Mine or Mustang Sally or Satisfaction or Hotel California : I even missed watching premier league football on TV at times and gave up supporting Chelsea (maybe just as well given their downturn in form . . . . and Drogba and Anelka are over here now, anyway!) and I really missed being able to watch Midsomer Murders on The Hallmark Channel which he got on his satellite TV late on Friday evenings. It really was a bit lonely then and there were a few occasions I must tell you that I cried myself to sleep but after a while I used to travel up to Beijing for the occasional long (sometimes very long!) weekend and that always compensated for things.

I must be honest and say I was also a bit jealous of him being on his own. Did I trust him? No, I certainly did not. Remember what I told you before about what I thought he might have got up to in my absences. Moreover, there was, I knew (well I do have a kind of insider knowledge!) plenty of temptation in the capital especially from the female Mongolian hordes who descended on the city in order to make easy bucks. (What rhymes with bucks?) Not a frightening sight as it was in the time of the early Chinese dynasties but rather a most welcome one especially to the expatriate men in the city and to some of the nouveau rich locals. However, I had to hope he could indeed resist temptation or at least do so in moderation. Mongolian women are dangerous : after all most of them I must admit are stunningly beautiful and certainly would make most men cream their pants. So I was concerned about the competition; who wouldn't be? But I had to control my jealousy and repeated to myself what the eye doesn't see . . . .

Sometimes, as I said I went and visited him. I had not been to Beijing since I was a little girl so I had no real memories of the place and really no preconceptions about it. It was good to see my country's capital city with its amazing architectural novelties. What made these visits even more enjoyable was that he now had a car, a nice, dark blue VW Passat, and so we got round to the usual places of interest—Tiananmen Square, Forbidden City, Summer Palace, Fragrant Hills, Great Wall at Simatai, The Lama Temple, Ghost Street, The Olympic Stadium, the Water Cube, Yashow Market—well, he liked that but I preferred Xin Kong Tiandi, Sanlitun North and South Village, The Place and the Financial district shopping malls! I even went to see the mausoleum of our once great leader, Mao Zedong, and even bought flowers (which get recycled of course—got to add to the government's income!) wherewith to strew beside his embalmed corpse lying in state. But if you ask me (and most others who visit there) it's a fake : couldn't really be preserved that well for the length of time he's been dead. Probably courtesy of Madame Tussaud's in London. Wait a minute : we Chinese can do fakes better than them! Thus initially some aspects of the weekends were very much being the tourist and, the other aspects were spent shopping of course. This is woman, after all! He had quickly picked up a great knowledge of the city and had no trouble driving round and after taking in the sights we got round to spending weekends just as we would have in Shanghai . . . . nice restaurants for brunches and dinners, bars with aggressive sounding rock bands, premier league football and yes, he had satellite in his apartment so we could watch Midsomer Murders, my favourite!

Sometimes he came back down to Shanghai. Then he would stay at one of the city's best hotels and I would share the weekend with him in luxury. All on expenses as he would say! Wow, this compensated for those lonely weeks and weekends! And the pattern of restaurants, bars etc continued.

The change brought about by his move therefore proved to be a difference in degree, not of kind. It took a bit of getting used to but it worked and we carried on contentedly while his sojourn there lasted.

All those tears were shed in vain . . . . well, not entirely.

Oh and we still enjoyed holidays together . . . .

PETER

Amazingly enough Dad showed some signs of improvement. Still confined to a wheelchair and has to have constant round the clock care and still a bit gaga for the majority of the time but there are moments of lucidity and he likes to be taken out an about a little more and I don't mean just strolls around our grounds—could be dangerous that anyway as if they weren't looking where they were going they might fall into the hole we made for the ice rink! No, he wants to go out and about around town and even I believe went to The Den of Iniquity a couple of times. He was probably mobbed by the women there! Not that he would be much use to them mind you! Those days have long gone for him. Guess that happens to all of us sometime or other. Quite a while to go for me yet though!

Since he does have these odd moments when he's just about compos mentis Mother felt she could leave him and take a short holiday so she decided to take those promised, and by now well overdue trips, to Russia. She had kept up correspondence via email and skype with a couple of guys and they were as good as their word so she packed her bags, went to the bank and off she went. Mind you, she took a chance flying on Aeroflot to Moscow! Well that was over a couple of months ago now and apart from the odd postcard and occasional text message she doesn't communicate often. Last I heard she said she's setting up business there with her two comrades and has had some very helpful business advice especially about visas for foreign workers from Yana, would you believe? Very helpful young lady that! And nice with it! She didn't say exactly what line of business she was in but my guess is that it must be something in social services : well, that's what Yana is involved in.

So it's a bit lonely around here, just me and Dad and his two nurses rattling around in this huge monstrosity of a building! Oh, by the way, I fired his original nurses. Didn't think they were up to scratch and amazingly enough I met two very nice young things at The Den of Iniquity and believe it or not they were nurses so . . . . Bob's your uncle as they say! Well, Dad has perked up occasionally as I said so I guess I made a good decision there. The wedding receptions and cadre parties still happen by the way so we survive money-wise but Mother took a considerable amount out of the coffers to start up her business in Russia of course and I must confess my life style has soaked up a lot of the readies I got from the Olympics. I spent my money on women and booze and wasted the rest : isn't that what they say?

I also haven't heard much from my wife and family in Bangkok recently. Keep meaning to go and see them but travel is an expensive business and I am happier staying at home—not literally of course. Got to get around ducking and diving as they say. I did get a phone call from her sometime ago now and she told me she was going for a holiday with the kids to England. Must be honest and say I don't know where she got the money for such a trip because I have got behind a bit with the allowance payments I usually send to her. But she never complained or even asked where the back payments were! She has sent me a postcard from London though and said her and the kids were having a great time. They were staying in a suburb called Chelsea and they loved going to watch the local team play in the premiership at Stamford Bridge. Never knew they were interested in football. Anyway, I am pleased for them and glad they are enjoying themselves. I did ask them to let me know when they were back in Bangkok as I really ought to do the husbandy thing and pay them a visit but they haven't replied yet so I guess the good times are still rolling in Chelsea! Long may they continue to do so as far as I'm concerned. It's good to know people are happy wherever they are.

So, got to get on with business. As you know, I was thinking about that Mongolian Troupe that Yana got for us for the Olympics but before I could make progress in that direction Michelle Wong cornered me on one of my visits to The Den of Iniquity. She is a great woman for business ideas but, as she told me herself, she needs the contacts and networking that only a smart and smooth entrepreneur like me can provide. Happy to oblige of course, if at all possible.

"Flattery will get you everywhere," I joked and she knowingly smiled back.

She explained about the, shall we call it mineral rush—well it's not about gold exactly—into Mongolia and that a lot of the development was being taken up by Australian companies. Had to get in quick. Definite business opportunity!

"You must have connections in Australia, Peter," she said. "After all you were educated there."

"True on both counts," I replied, "but into mineral mining? Honestly I cannot think off hand of any one of my mates who went into that line of business. But I will try, that's a promise."

"Don't just try, Peter, try hard," she replied. "Please think about it and get back to me. There's money in them thar Mongolian deserts," she said in a quasi-American accent as she left.

But she came back quite quickly and introduced me to two, stunningly beautiful Mongolian ladies, Nandia and Anna, and just before she left me with them she said, "Oh by the way, Jenny Jing's also interested and can do a whole load of real estate deals if we can get something going up there."

Having Michelle and Jenny as business partners was certainly an incentive for me to put my thinking cap on about contacts from my old school in Oz.

However, there was no direct contact I could think of who had gone into the mining business. Sheep farming, surf boarding, cricket, Aussie rules, hotel management, travel companies, life guarding, back packing, acting in some dreadful TV soaps, a handful, a very small handful I might add, even went on to Uni, but mining? Seemed to have hit a dead end. Had to turn to my school year books. Yes, got those year after year but rarely if ever looked at them just piled them up in a corner of my hardly used office in Neuschwanstein where they gathered mildew (Chinese are not noted for putting in damp courses) and dust. So I got hold of them and flicked through the ones that hadn't got so much mildew that they could still be flicked through to see what I could find. Nothing much came up except for a James Parkinson who had gained a scholarship to read minerology at Melbourne Uni. Not just got a place at Uni but gained a scholarship indeed?

Must have been a nerd, I thought to myself. He was not in my year group but a couple of years below me and truth to tell I could not remember him at all. Well, I didn't have much to do with guys outside my chums in my year.

Next I followed up on Google. There's a lot of James Parkinsons there : if you don't believe me try it and see. But sure enough, Doctor James Parkinson (Doctor indeed—definitely a nerd!) from Melbourne Uni featured quite highly and he had made it to the dizzy heights of Professor of Geology and Minerology at Adelaide Uni and was .... wait for it! .... advisor to The Western Australian Mineral and Conglomerates Company. This was literally and metaphorically a turn up for the books. Was I the right man to make such contacts or was I the right man to make such contacts? Great piece of research, eh?

But how was I to approach him? I never even acknowledged his presence when we were at school together and he would hardly have remembered me. Old school tie, however, means as much to us as it does to guys with much older school ties in the UK. It would have to serve as an introduction if nothing else.

I eventually managed to contact him on the blower. Took a bit of time getting through but amazingly enough after my briefest of introductions by way of our old school he actually did remember me. And not only me but a lot of my mates in my year group.

"You guys were truly legends in your own playtimes," he recalled. "Staff and governors were always on about you bringing the school into disrepute but to juniors below you like me and the rest, we were envious of your drunken binges, cocaine snorting, glue sniffing, weed smoking, pill popping or whatever and your conquests of women and your general disregard for school rules and regulations. Heroes, you were, make no mistake about it. We could never hope to live up to your high standards in those respects. Certainly never emulated since, I am pretty sure of that! We often wondered why you never got expelled . . . . but money counts, doesn't it?"

His recollections were quite a recommendation, I think you'll admit. I must admit his words almost brought a tear to my eye. Happy days! Imagine, him remembering me when I had no idea of who he was and couldn't even be sure if I'd ever clapped eyes on him at school. Just goes to show!

So it was we got talking about his area of interest, minerals and mineral rights. He agreed Mongolia was ripe for development but indicated any company would definitely be in need of partners and investment to get it going.

"Meiwente," I said but I doubt he understood.

I outlined prospects to him and managed to convince him so that he agreed to come over to Beijing and meet up with Jenny and Michelle and me. Naturally, I also did promise him a good time in Beijing. A very good time.

"Something along the lines of what I and my mates achieved at school, I promise you, James," I joked.

"Ah, well, in that case, I am definitely up for it," he rejoined without any further hesitation.

When I told Michelle she was impressed I could tell and agreed to make sure James had the very best of times when he came to China. So all was set for a new business deal and probably one that would be bigger and better than all the rest put together. I was really excited about it so I did briefly outline it to Dad when he was in one of his more lucid moods but sadly since then he has had a bit of a relapse. A real pity as I would liked him to have felt he really was a part of it. Maybe once we have all the agreements set up he will perk up again. I certainly hope so.

Pity Nandia and Anna aren't nurses . . . .

WU DABIN &
JIANG SHULIN

It's a bit of a sad time for us. Mr Harding has gone off to Beijing. That's brought some changes for us. Not too bad ones we're pleased to say but handling change is not easy and things were going along ever so smoothly with Mr Harding in charge at the school and with Ms Fu looking after him in his apartment. Well, we cannot complain really. After all we haven't had to put up with anything like our parents had to in the 60s and 70s with the Cultural Revolution and all that. There were so many changes then for them they never knew whether they were coming or going. In the end of course it was seen for what it all was : bullshit! Then again, more recently they've had to put up with the new city developments in China after Deng Xiao Ping's opening up. Sometimes they are frightened to go out because of all the new buildings, underpasses, elevated highways, shopping malls, new parks and gardens etc that have shot up because they worry about getting lost! Sat nav's not much use in China in its state of development at the moment so it's no good thinking that would help.

So, the changes? Well, no work as an ayi for Mr Harding now but I do now work one day a week for Ms Fu in her new apartment. I still also do work for Daisy, of course. It's a bit of a come down from the residence she shared with Mr Harding in Xintiandi but it's smart and tidy and together we keep it spick and span, ship shape and Bristol fashion and all that. It's also in a good location towards the middle of Nanjing Xi Lu so she's got all the shops and restaurants she needs around her. She heads off to Beijing on some weekends and always brings me something back from there. Usually some tasty delicacies! What a kind, lovely young lady she is. Over Chinese pu er tea and the occasional cream cake which we have at times on my days I go round to her place she also regales me with stories of the capital : it sounds an exciting place and she actually says apart from the cost of housing and apartments it's a cheaper place to live than Shanghai! Who would have believed it?

As for the changes affecting Mr Wu?..Let him tell you.

When I was at the school Mr Harding treated me and everyone equally. No side or airs or graces with him so the staff relationships, by that I mean us ancillary and maintenance workers got on ever so well with all the teachers, the students and the parents and we all respected each other. A truly collegiate approach. We all went about our jobs professionally and God was in Heaven and sausages for breakfast : isn't that what you say? Truly, a great sense of camaraderie pervaded the place. It was almost tangible and I am sure visitors to the school noticed it, could feel it even. All this thanks to his great management style.

Not long after he left in comes the new incumbent. New broom sweeps clean is what he said. What a difference! He was into ordering us about, we never got invited to staff do's any more, our holidays were cut, no more overtime pay and we were made to feel like servants in the white man's world. Second class citizens. Back to the opium war days, the days of treaty ports and French, German concession areas etc. No dogs! No Chinese! It seems colonialism is endemic in some Brits. He also made sweeping changes in the staff management within the school. So it was that the people who didn't understand anything were now put in charge of the people who did! Teaching staff weren't happy about things nor were quite a few parents and the best of them stayed friends with us; but others? Theirs not to reason why, I guess, and everyone in the end protects their own interests so the school became a place of disaffection. Whilst I was good at my work and enjoyed doing what I did, I and many others, now lacked what I would call job satisfaction. Yes, we all work for money but that can never be the be all and end all. To go into work and find everything and nearly everyone miserable and depressing as was now the case was really too much to bear. I became as you would say totally pissed off with this state of affairs. At times like these, our only insurance is ourselves.

Who was it said when dictatorship is a fact, revolution is a duty? Not Chairman Mao though he did have a lot to say about revolution, that's for sure! And not Lao Tse though he did write The Art of War with some very useful advice therein. Well, at first the situation made me so angry that I felt like inaugurating a rebellion against the dictatorial, foreign devils. Bit like the Boxer rebellion at the start of the 20th century but we Chinese have learned from bitter experience that rebellions or revolutions whatever you like to call them are, to quote the late, great Chairman Mao, not a picnic and anyway, I am not an aggressive man. Indeed, we Chinese are not an aggressive nation, despite what some countries in the rest of the world think. C'mon, even your Monty Python sang about us being always friendly and ready to please! Oh and they said we are cute and cuddly too! Well, to continue, the best means of attack is defence and it always best to play the enemy at its own game. Sad that it had now come down to me thinking of the school where I'd spent so many happy, industrious working hours as an enemy.

Fortunately, however, the international school developments had not entirely come to an end and a new establishment was opening up in Shanghai. I knew it might not be as good as under Mr Harding's management but it was different : it was a bilingual school, not a strictly British School so it could accept local Chinese students. Many of us defected and so we are now in the new school and under its new management. And, to be honest, it's not as good as under Mr Harding but it is so much better than what the old school had become under its new regime. Good riddance to that.

Mr Harding still stays in touch and when he comes down to Shanghai he will arrange to take us (not just me and the missus but quite a few of his former ancillary staff) out to dinner and we recount and relive, at least in our imaginations and with advantages, old times. Fond memories indeed. We are hoping he may come back to Shanghai full time and set up something else in the educational world here in which case I think we'd all be ready to defect again and we know he would offer us the opportunity to do so but of one thing I am sure, he would not encourage us to break contracts. A stickler for rules and regulations he certainly was in the nicest possible way of course.

Another change is coming up soon for us but I'll hand you back to my wife for that.

Yes, Dong Dong will be going to take her Gao Kao later this year. That's the entrance examination to get into university. The higher score you get the better university you can attend. A bit of a dogmatic system but got to go along with it. It's important she keeps her nose to the grindstone and gets a good result. We'd like her to make it to Fudan if possible so that she will study in Shanghai where we work and we will be able to see her a little more often. So soon I intend to take at least 9 months out and go back to Anhui in order to stay with her and make sure she does well. Daisy won't be too pretty pleased I guess but I think she'll understand. Dong Dong's paternal grandparents have done quite a good job—though as I previously said I do have some reservations about the way they've gone about things—but it's now time for me to step in. This is the Tiger mother speaking but many of us are like that in China. We want what is best for our children and the way forward for them to move up the ladder of success lies in educational results. I think that idea is something the west has abandoned. It is interesting that the UK curriculum is probably thought more of abroad and by foreign nationals than it is rated in its own country. Guess it's true what your good book says : No prophet is accepted in his own country!

Of course, I will be able to keep an eye on Gary when I am in Anhui as well and hopefully make sure he doesn't become a hooligan, despite some of the traits he has been showing of late, like a lot of western youths his age. I know boys will be boys and as I have said before I don't expect him to reach the academic heights like his sister but if Mr Wu can get a good job from all the trades he is master of then Gary should be able to do so as well. We should all be able to succeed in our own spheres.

Even being a mother, or a father for that matter, is a lot of people to be.

FU

Mr Harding—John to me—is, as I have said far too loving and too generous to his family and friends. We all, and I readily admit it self-included, take advantage of this. However, I have tried to tell him he should be more careful with his money and he should think about the future. When I do this he laughs. First he reminds me he is from a working class background and he says you can take a man out of the working class but not the working class out of the man. He told me though his family were not well off there was a lot of happiness at home and they always had a roof over their heads and food on the table. He also told me when he was 14 he got his first semi-professional musical engagement and in that week, just playing in a show at the local theatre in the evenings, he earned more than his father did working a 44 hour a week! Then he goes on and reminds me life's not a dress rehearsal and as he says, "No one gets out alive!" and he tells of a joke cartoon he saw in one of his sister's magazines when he was young. The cartoon he said showed a solicitor reading a will to the family gathered in the office and the caption was, "I, Joe Bloggs, (or whoever!) being of sound mind spent it all!"

Well that's his philosophy on money so he says. But I do wish he would be a bit more considerate of himself in this respect. Of course, this is so very different an approach to money compared with us Chinese. We do care about the future and we do save. That's probably why China is doing OK in the international finance markets whilst America and the Eurozone countries are, pardon my French, in the shit. Interesting, isn't it that they now come and want to borrow of us! What is it you say : look after the pennies and the pounds will take care of themselves? Didn't do a very good job of looking after the pennies, did you? Or in Greece's terms was that drachmas? Well they're in the Eurozone, (at the time of writing this!) so I should say, the euros! Borrowing from China should remind you of Antonio and Shylock in Merchant of Venice shouldn't it? Perhaps we should demand our pound of flesh?

As for Mr Harding—John to me—on the other hand he spends a kind of schizophrenic life as in his work he says he behaves like a tyrant. Sure, Mr Wu will confirm he rules with a rod of iron but treats everyone in the school equally. He has another cartoon framed in his office which I've seen. It shows a galley ship with all the slaves on board sweating and rowing and in the middle is the galley master whip in hand and looking like a really nasty piece of work. The caption reads (one slave talking to the mate beside him), "He has this way of motivating people!" Well, I know that's not really Mr Harding's—John to me—way of working but he is a stickler for rules, I do know that. All in all a real character and someone I can't help admitting and loving in my own way.

Well, some of his money he has kindly spent on me taking me away to faraway places with strange sounding names. However, the country I really like is England and very fortunately for me he has taken me there twice. In order to do so he has managed to adopt some Chinese habits in his time here and lying is definitely one of them. I should say in China it's not regarded as lying exactly but it's more like telling people what they want to hear or perhaps what they need to hear. White lies, I think you call them and you have a phrase, "economical with the truth" which I think aptly applies to us.

The first trip we did we flew from Hong Kong. He said he was going there on business and we did stay one night there during which he purchased a few postcards and mailed them to a few relatives and friends thereby adding corroborative detail to his story : and he did the same when we returned. The second time he flew home and stayed with his family at home initially but he had indicated he had conferences to attend in London and

Oxford. I flew over by myself, he picked me up in London and we did a wonderful tour of the south and the west and in May when the weather was really fine. I then flew back on my own whilst he returned as they say to the bosom of his family.

I did so like England that I would like to go back there again. I remember the first time I saw cows and sheep in your fields right next to the roadside. I asked Mr Harding—John to me—to stop the car so I could get out and take a photo.

"No chance," he said. "We're on a motorway and you only stop on the hard shoulder in an emergency."

I was really upset by that and we almost had a serious fall out about it. For me it was an emergency! Anyway, more to the point, in China we stop on the roads when and where we want to, any time, any place. Here everything 'belongs to the people' (check out our use of *renmin*) so what we do and how we use everything is O.K. Anyway, later on when we got off the motorway he did pull over so I did get my photos of the sheep and the cows in the fields.

Then in London I got a great photo in the metro, or underground or subway as you call it. Everyone standing on the right on the escalators so people could go past up or down on the left. What a sense of order! It's everyone for themselves getting in or out of the trains and going up or down the escalators in our cities. On intercity train journeys, too, you could buy return tickets and get on trains at any time, an impossibility with most rail journeys given the number of travelers in China. It's a great system and one I would love us to adopt but probably as I have implied, a bit impractical for us.

We visited Portsmouth and went in some superb restaurants and, as a seaside city, there's was plenty of seafood available. But it was dead fish, crabs, lobsters etc. No chance of selecting from live specimens in the tanks like in China. What a disappointment! As a result the fish was a bit tasteless and, for all I know might have been deep frozen for ages before we got it. Mind you, your fish and chips, one of your national dishes, seems odd to me as it you seem to go out of your way to make the fish not even taste like fish! What's the point of that? Your chips are pretty good though!

Oh and lovers, sometimes even of the same sex, (well I assume they were lovers but I guess you never know) kissing and cuddling in the street, on the trains or on buses! How romantic but definitely a bit indelicate and improper I think. I turned my eyes away when I saw such unions at first and even though I realised it was acceptable practice I couldn't help feeling embarrassed whenever I saw it. Such open and public displays of affection are a bit taboo in China. Mind you, given the cold and damp weather in England maybe it's also a way of keeping warm since, unlike us in China, where when cold weather comes we dress up like Michelin Tyre Man, it seems you almost dress the same whatever the weather.

By the way, I felt even more embarrassed when I kept seeing photos of topless ladies in one of your tabloid newspapers every day. I guess there must be some kind of crime epidemic among young, attractive females that makes them end up in the newspapers every day of the week. It seems the reporters are doing a good job in tracking down these female criminals but the police can't be doing very much as it seems to be a continuing problem.

Talking of tabloid newspapers. It is strange that your media, especially the tabloids, seem to control (perhaps even select?) your government. In China it's very much the government that controls (perhaps even selects?) the media. But then do you, or we for that matter, write what we believe or believe what we write?

To return to the subject of inappropriate dress (Did we ever leave it I ask myself? having just touched on the photos of young ladies in the tabloids)—Mr Harding—John to me—took me to a premier league football match in London. Chelsea v Liverpool. Wow it was exciting but the crowds—worse than at Carrefour in Gubei, Shanghai, on a Sunday afternoon and that's saying something! And all kept under control by policemen on horseback. I doubt such crowd control would have prevailed at Tiananmen Square in 1989! Tanks before horses there! Anyway, I could not believe it, for there we were on a dull, damp, dreary December Saturday afternoon and some supporters just wore short-sleeved, football shirt tops and some even were naked down to the waist. Some, admittedly did have scarves but they used them as kind of flags or pennants holding and swaying them above their heads when they chanted and not using them for warmth in any way. Very strange.

Oh and I did so like the West Country. All those lovely villages exactly like in my favourite programme, Midsomer Murders. A bit odd though that many of the houses have roofs of grass (thatch I think you call it!) and yet they are more expensive than houses with tiled, slate roofs. Our Chinese comrades in the countryside here would be delighted if their humble abodes, which also have grass roofs, were valued in that way. They'd then get more compensation for them from the government when it decides to move them on to live in a new tower block in order to build a new airport, housing compound, office block, subway line, Olympic stadium, shopping mall or whatever where they currently dwell!

I must compliment you on your taxi services in your cities. Your taxi drivers, by the way, are the bees' knees. They actually know where to go once you tell them your destination. Not like our taxi drivers. You have to give them not only your destination but you have to navigate them to it. I must compliment you foreigners because all of you take the trouble to learn taxi-driver's Chinese otherwise you'd never get around our cities. No good putting sat nav in our cabs : cities are in a constant state of flux and anyway our dummies wouldn't know how to make it work.

I've pointed out some differences between our countries but we also have a lot in common. For example we have 56 ethnic groups living in China and, by the looks of things in England, you must have something like a similar number living here. You love animals especially dogs (A dog is a man's best friend, as you say!) and so do we! Here, though, we have a bit of a difference in kind : because we love to eat them, you love to keep them as pets. Vive la difference! I know that many English people when they come to China and eat at a Chinese restaurant are amused by some of our dishes, for example, ducks' tongues, beggar's chicken, dan dan noodles, snake and fish-head soup, sea urchin etc. But how about your dishes? Bubble and squeak, pigs' trotters, fisherman's pie, shepherd's pie, upside down cake, tripe and onions, jellied eels, beef Wellington, black pudding, spotted dick, haggis? Oops, sorry to insert what I believe is a famous Scottish dish at the end there! Then there's the regional accents. You have the Geordies, Cockney, Scots, Liverpuddlian, Estuary English etc; we have Shanghaiese,

Wuxiese, Cantonese (in Guandong and all places south!) and have you heard and tried to understand the guttural sounds of the Beijingers?

I certainly loved your famous old universities, Oxford and Cambridge. It was also so good to see your war on drugs being emphasised in those educational establishments so frequently. A good idea to keep reminding young people who are probably more susceptible to getting involved in drugs about the dangers of possible addiction. And the polite way you phrase your warnings : Please keep off the grass. So typical of the English, friendly, polite, courteous, not wishing to give any offence, just like Mr Harding—John to me! Here again there's a similarity between us. Even your former Cambridge and Oxford graduates, the Monty Python Group, commented on how polite and friendly we Chinese are. What was it they sang?

I like Chinese . . . . .

They're always friendly and they're willing to please.

So true, don't you think? Just like you English!

(And, by way of emphasizing the point I have just made, by the way, we have no hard feelings that it was you who introduced opium to us in the 19th century and that helped really fuck up our country for quite a few decades!)

Yes, England is a lovely country and the English charming people. Yes, charming, indeed! That's the word

I am looking for. As I say I do want to go back there again and maybe journey further north this time. Must sweet talk Mr Harding—John to me! I am sure he will oblige. Maybe get into Bonnie Scotland! Perhaps I'd find more differences but also some similarities between the Chinese and Scots. I've been told they speak a rougher kind of English and there's even a different language called Gaelic that's difficult to understand and that the men wear skirts. Now that is strange! I hope that doesn't have the implications that readily spring to mind! But, as they say in France, Chacun a son gout!

Now France . . . . that's another interesting country.

BILL

The Chinese invented writing. They also invented printing. Once you invent writing and printing then you have to invent something to write on and print on. So they invented paper. Once you invent paper, you increase your vocabulary and I am sure the words duplicate, triplicate, copy, facsimile, foolscap, quarto, A4 etc etc were also invented in China as they seem to have a love affair with writing, printing but most of all, paper. If you don't believe me, come with me on a brief visit for a few relatively simple transactions in a Chinese Bank. Doesn't matter which bank—they seem to be in plentiful supply of them (well, they do seem to have accumulated a lot of wealth recently and now effectively part own America and are on their way to owning Europe perhaps in its entirety)—the transactions are handled in the same way in all banks.

The first thing you notice is you have to get a ticket to get in a queue and wait to be seen just like at a deli counter in one of our supermarkets. You will find out why in a while. Well, I say in a while but that could mean anything from 20 minutes to a few hours. Sorry, but I should have said it is advisable to bring a book to read, a crossword to complete, your mobile phone on which to play games or just surf the world news on your IPAD or whatever while you wait : time passes in these places not like an ever flowing stream but more like the Chinese water torture, drip by delayed drip . . . . drip . . . . drip! Thinks : maybe the Chinese invented time as well! So, after a while your number comes up, it's displayed on a screen and also announced in Chinese and English, and you go to the counter.

Despite China's entry into the WTO, IMF or whatever and their massive expansion of tourism and the influx of foreign companies, you will find you will get a better standard of English from a Chinese barista in Starbucks or Costa Coffee than you are likely to get from bank tellers, or for that matter from most bank employees. However, along comes one who does speakee some Yingouish and can help out. Mind you, the translation process adds considerably to the transaction time! So here's the transaction:

$3,000 [USD] has been transferred from my offshore account in the UAE to my Chinese Bank account. I want to use it to pay off my Chinese Bank Visa card.

Well, I say $3,000 has been transferred to my account. In Chinese terms it hasn't yet. What has happened is that a transfer has been recorded but the sum of money seems to exist in the ether, cyber space, the electronic universe or wherever and the first thing I have to do is get it into my account. Now we start the paper trail!

Paper 1 : Inward remittance advice. This is a red form about A5 size indicating the transfer. It has my name, account number and the details of the transferring bank. It is also officially now 'chopped' with the bank's official stamp.

Paper 2 : Reporting Form for receipts from abroad. This is a blue form, which has to be signed by me and again officially chopped by the bank. It is two pieces of paper A4 size and inserts all the previous details from Paper 1 but also has the addition of my mobile phone number which I have to provide.

Paper 3 : Deposit slip. This records the $3,000 as now being officially in my account. It is red and it is also chopped.

Paper 4 : Withdrawal slip. I need to pay the USD to my visa card separately from the RMB Chinese currency. Blue withdrawal slip for $2,000 signed for by me and chopped by the bank.

Paper 5 : Deposit Slip. Red and indicating $2,000 now credited to my visa card. Signed and chopped as per usual.

Paper 6 : Withdrawal slip (blue) for $1,000 being the remainder from the first dollar transfer. Signed and chopped as per usual.

Paper 7 : Deposit Interests Bill slip indicating the balance has received no interest. Signed and chopped as per usual.

Paper 8 : Exchange memo indicating the withdrawal (Paper 6) is now being changed into RMB. Signed and chopped as per usual.

Paper 9 : Red deposit slip for the RMB into my account. Signed and chopped as per usual.

Paper 10 : Blue transfer slip for RMB payment to my visa card. Signed and chopped as per usual.

So I now have a wad of 11 pieces of paper (I can count, check 2 above!) of various shapes and sizes and the bank has duplicate and sometimes triplicate copies of these as well and since some of mine are mere tear off slips, theirs are considerably larger and bulkier. So on average 3+ pieces of paper per transaction!

You will, as I have said before, see the same duplication, triplication or whatever process in their shopping malls of course. Didn't I say they have a love affair with paper? Now do you believe me?

Imagine the storage space for all of this! No wonder there's so much construction work everywhere. Imagine the fire risk for all of this! We must hope they are insured!

Oh, by the way, had you looked at your watch when you sat down to do these transactions and then looked when all was done you would have seen about 40 minutes of your life had slipped by. Add to that your waiting time . . . . and time passes quickly when you are having fun. Well, I guess in China what you have to do is shrug your shoulders and say, "Well, it would have passed anyway!" And it would have I suppose. Bit like Waiting for Godot, isn't it? But Beckett clearly never visited China otherwise he would have used this scenario in his play instead of the verbal exchanges to pass the time.

By the way, if you forgot to bring your passport (ID card for the locals) go directly to home, do not dare attempt to wait in the optimistic hope you will be seen and certainly do not expect to be served. [It's not unlike going to the airport to catch a plane . . . . including the waiting and delay time!]

Have a nice day!

And P.S. if you want another paper chase try getting or changing your mobile phone number at China Mobile! Or, alternatively, fail to register your presence within 30 days of arrival and see what the Public Security Bureau can do by way of de-forestisation.

JENNY JING

Had a great time shopping at Sanlitun North Village! Cost an arm and a leg but things have already started to look up on the minerals rush business! So, although the bank account is slightly depleted at present it is only a temporary setback.

Michelle managed to get Peter to get a useful contact, James Parkinson, for us just as she said she would and he came over from Australia and we entertained him royally! We took him to the best restaurants, showed him all the wonderful, historical and modern architectural sights of our impressive, capital city Beijing, took him to acrobatic shows and concerts (definitely did not bore him with Chinese opera!) and put him up at The Peninsula which is pretty swish and five star plus of course! (Got quite a good rate there thanks to one my contacts. Well, we all have to do out bit.) Imagine though! Peter was wanting him to stay at Neuschwanstein but we managed to dissuade him from making such a gaffe! He was a trifle miffed by this saying old school chums should stick together and have a chance to enjoy each other's company and his place had plenty of spare rooms and anyway it would be cheaper. (Well, truth to tell he had agreed to foot all the bills so his thinking was understandable but certainly not excusable!) Michelle managed to convince him otherwise and capped her persuasion by the reception laid on for him and his chum at The Den of Iniquity. By all accounts, this not only persuaded Peter but it proved to be the deal clincher for James. This is Man! They wear their brains etc. I did not go to that event for obvious reasons but Michelle did let me know all about it. Well, a bit of vicarious living is not so bad, is it? So it looks like I will be off for a few treks to Mongolia over the forthcoming months courtesy of Peter's finance, naturally. Should be interesting!

Meanwhile, Dongdong came on a brief visit to stay with us. Lala convinced me in allowing this to happen by telling me Dong dong was going to be sitting her Gao Kao at school this year and therefore would not be able to get such a break for a long time to come as she would be studying so hard. So, wanting to please my daughter (what mother doesn't want to do that?) I agreed and so she came up for 10 days.

She was a very nice girl and had been well brought up but, oh dear, her sense of dress and style left something—actually quite a lot really—to be desired. Having said that her wardrobe was very limited and seeing what she had brought at first I thought she only intended to stay for about two days. I had to remind myself that she was not used to living in a tier one city and therefore would not know about and could not come up to such standards of most of us who have that privilege. I guess that in the provinces, *It's life, Jim, but not as we know it,* is the best that can be said. A bit of an embarrassment as far as I was concerned but Lala seemed totally unphased by it all. Well, there's no accounting for taste, is there?

I did discretely ask her about how her England trip was financed and she told me that it had in part been paid for by the Principal of the school where her father worked and for whom her mother was an ayi. Very kind of him, I thought, and lucky you, young lady. An interesting gesture but in my opinion a somewhat old fashioned foreign devil ruse to ingratiate himself with the locals. Am I being over cynical? I personally think not. Anyway, to be fair to her she had made excellent use of the freebie holiday as her English was really very good indeed. Better than Lala's for sure so I made a mental note to follow through on that after she left and I feel I may well afford to send Lala back there this coming summer or I may even get her a private tutor. Well, I might be galavanting around Mongolia so she will need to be being looked after somewhere or other and by someone or other.

As I said, she was obviously well brought up and was very polite and thankful for us putting her up and taking her round the city. She certainly expressed her gratitude for the lovely bedroom we gave her (the sheets were changed daily!), for the trips out in my lovely Audi car and for all the nice food we gave her at home and the restaurants we took her to. She seemed embarrassed by the latter saying she rarely dined out and when she did so tended to go to the local restaurants which as she agreed with me were crowded, smoke filled and pretty raucous places and where the smell of burnt sesame cooking oil together with the aroma (can it be called that?) of bai jiu basically told you the kind of meal you were going to have before you had it! So the refinement of such places as Middle 8th Restaurant and Karaiya Spice House here came as a surprise to her. She did feel more at home when we took her for a meal in Ghost Street though. Well, the restaurants there are crowded, smoke filled and pretty raucous places and where the smell of burnt sesame cooking oil together with the aroma (can it be called that?) of bai jiu basically tells you the kind of meal you are going to have before you have it! So that was a labour of love, I can tell you!

She enjoyed the sights of Beijing. I think it's always a good thing that we should visit and get to know a bit about our wonderful capital city and its history. So we did do the touristy bit—we went to see the Olympic stadium—rather something of a faded beauty there now but it did its bit to attract the visitors in 2008. Still it makes money as they charge 50RMB for visitors and they certainly get plenty. The water cube's now a water theme park and I think it pulls in more visitors than it ever got when the Olympic swimming was held there. Much more profitable too! Houhai and Behai Parks are always worth a visit but to be honest I prefer to go there in Winter when all the people are skating on the ice—though there's always some hardy folks swimming there even then, would you believe? It's a pity there are so many bars and clubs now in those places—they may make it look bright and sparkling at night, glamorous almost, but in my opinion they seriously lower the tone. Still, Michelle has a club there and that sure brings in the cash for her.

Of course The Great Wall at Simatai (by far the best bit!), The Ming Tombs, The Summer Palace, The Forbidden City are all de rigeur and she really did seem interested not only in the places but all the history they conveyed. Really lapped it up! Lala seemed a bit bored and disinterested by it and complained every now and then. Must say that upset me a bit because in some of these places it was her first visit too. Again I made a mental note of that and maybe there too she might need some extra history lessons in the future—help her understand and then she may well show more interest.

Maybe get her a private tutor for that as well. Of course we also went to pay homage to Chairman Mao, sanctified as he is in his mausoleum : still long, long queues there which shows his popularity even to this day. Still, quite a moving experience as well. Strange that after we went there Dongdong actually asked me was it real. Was it real? I had to do a double take, believe me! She seemed to think that embalming a body and being able to preserve it for such a length of time was pretty near scientifically impossible without it deteriorating. As she pointed out, even Egyptian mummies tend to end up in a pretty bad way. Of course I assured her about modern techniques and the greatness of Chinese medical expertise in that respect but she still seemed unconvinced. I also reminded her that Lenin's corpse had been preserved for a much longer time that Chairman Mao's. It did not seem to convince her. No doubt she'll be asking me soon if the Long March actually did take place! Lala, sadly, wasn't the slightest bit interested in the visit or the discussion! Well, on reflection, young people ask and say the strangest things at times, don't they?

So her visit passed and I felt very pleased everything had gone smoothly. I know Lala would like to reciprocate the visit sometime, possibly after Dongdong has sat her Gao Kao. Lala seems very keen and Dongdong certainly was enthusiastic about having her stay but I am not so sure. May do Lala some good to see how the other half lives though. We will have to wait and see.

Well, mustn't dwell on the past. That's the worst place in which to live. Mongolia calls. I'll be meeting with James, Peter and Michelle for dinner at The Peninsula over the weekend. Peter's paying of course and we will make some firm dates for starting our projects. Must say, James is quite an interesting man . . . . might be worth getting to know him better.

PETER

Never thought I'd be doing the entrepreneurial bit in Mongolia! But that's me. Not one to let the grass grow under his feet! Got to keep the wheels of business and finance turning! So we are going to be up and running in the next few months and James has got an Aussie Company, Tio Rinto, who are very interested in the deal and willing to get moving with us. Smart man!

Jenny's handling real estate and she says she's even going to get an international school built there. Michelle is organizing facilities, entertainment etc as part of the development—well, having some macho men over from 'down under' means we have to lay on something by way of after hours diversions. James is doing all the company bit, five year business plan, due diligence and all that, and I'm doing the initial finance. It's quite a steep outlay but well worth it. James convinced me—he really is a smart lad and not the nerd I first thought him to be!—that to prove it was all going to be worthwhile I should show a fair bit of the investment myself. That, as he rightly said, convinced the company and others that we meant business. The outlay then is big but the return on investment, of course, that's much bigger! As James said to me, "You know it makes sense." And indeed I do.

However, must confess to you I have had to do a bit of jiggery pokery to get the initial investment myself. Tried to talk to Dad about everything and saying we could re-mortgage our wonderful castle in order to do this but I didn't get through to him. He actually went apoplectic, had a massive fit and had to be taken to hospital. Actually he's still in hospital even now. I do try to visit him as often as possible but that's not easy with all the business I have to transact. Moreover, he's really not responding well to treatment and the visits sometimes are a bit of a waste of time as all I do is sit there and talk to him without any response whatsoever. It's sad to see him in a vegetative state like this especially as we are on the verge of a big financial breakthrough with the Mongolian project.

Now, where was I? Yes, jiggery pokery. I telephoned Mum of course when Dad was hospitalized and explained the situation. I had hoped she would be able to come over and visit him but she said she just had no time at all at present as work was so demanding. To be fair to her, to come all that way and just sit there watch him vegetate would not really make her journey worth it. What could she do for him? However, she was more than interested in the Mongolian project and said she would get back to me.

True to her word she did phone very soon afterwards and she said she would arrange the finance subject to various agreements related to the castle which she would draw up with her Russian colleagues. I am not sure what has happened in every respect but I did sign (actually 'forge' Dad's signature) on some deeds both in Chinese and Russian. Well, I didn't actually 'forge' his signature I just put the pen in his hand and moved it—his hand, not the pen!—so he could sign. That's not forgery, is it? He was totally comatose at the time but I don't think that matters really, does it? Mum certainly said it was OK but she did advise me not to have any witnesses present. So it was all behind the screens in the hospital of course! That was odd because technically his signature had, as it said on the form, to be witnessed by an independent third party. Well, I had to cover that somehow. Didn't want to get caught out on what is after all, let's be honest, a mere technicality. I was all for persuading Nadia to put her monica on it but Mum (after my insistence that we must get someone) came out with a better idea. "Got to have someone totally independent," she said and in that sense Nadia would certainly not do. Too easy to connect her with me. So she got a guy called Zhou Ho Li to meet me and sign on the dotted line. I had never seen him before (and haven't seen him since). How Mum got hold of him I have really no idea. I don't know and honestly don't want to know. Well, it worked a treat anyway. Realised the necessary capital and that's what business is all about, isn't it?

Shortly after the deed was done, the money arrived. It was sent in roubles and that caused a problem at the bank—ugh, the paperwork involved! But once it was changed into RMB there was no problem. We did our sums, dividing up the allocations to the various parties for their part in the scheme of things and it seems even Zhou Ho Li had to get a cut via a transfer to an offshore account—well, can't really deny him that since he did oblige as they say! Next it was off to Mongolia, Ulaanbaatar to get things going properly by meeting up with James and the Aussie crew. And, I hope Michelle has started to get the entertainment organized up there : I have, after all, already given her the necessary 'readies.'

Ulaanbaatar . . . ? Enough said. Jenny was right. Could do with totally knocking down and completely rebuilding and, interestingly enough, in some ways that's what Jenny intended to do. Not entirely of course but there was plenty of scope for razing some buildings to the ground and starting afresh and the government there didn't seem to mind. Don't think they would know what a preservation order is anyway. What is it someone said about us Chinese? We're not only good at destroying the past but also good at building the future! Ah, so true.

MICHELLE

It's good that things are getting underway in Mongolia. Pretty straightforward really. Working with Peter, or should I say getting him to work for us, is hardly hard work; almost enjoyable, certainly funny haha at times since it is hard to believe someone can be so dense. Maybe that comes from being educated in Australia. Apologies to my antipodean clients! We Chinese can not only take you foreigners for a ride but we obviously have a way with our own brethren at times as well! How else do you make money? That's what's called business acumen, isn't it?

My businesses are doing well and I have, as you have learned, always had a way of networking through them. Business has got to work for you as much as you have to work for it! It's a kind of re-cycling! Part of the circle of life? So it was that recently a new guy turned up at Den of Iniquity. Initially he seemed a bit different from the usual clientele. A really dapper chap and a bit shy with it. He came along rather well suited and booted and at first I thought he would be a bit of a bore, but not a bit of it.

Naturally as a new kid on the block I greeted him and we got chatting. What a truly engaging man he turned out to be. So well educated and a great depth of personality beneath that shy exterior. I was only too happy to spend a fair bit of time with him and we shared a complimentary bottle of red house wine on our first meeting. He drank most of it as I, of course, have to keep a clear head in my line of work—well, until after hours (if there can be said to be such a thing in my line of work!) He seemed well capable of taking his drink, I might add. A good sign.

John Harding. That's the man's name. Extremely well educated—ex UK public (joke?) school (Malvern) and Bristol and Oxford universities. He had set up an international school in Shanghai—not an easy job by any stretch of the imagination given the nature of the educational authorities down there, not to mention their city government—and was now working on projects in Beijing. Just the right guy to advise me about my daughter's education. Wasn't he just? I'm always looking for the main chance. So naturally I tapped him about this. He was very helpful and has already put me in touch with some of the right schools in the UK. Not only that, but he has contacts and a bit of guanxi (he calls it old school tie!) with some of them so he has helped support my applications on Elisabeth's behalf. Kind, considerate and helpful—typical English gentleman. So, all's well in that direction as well.

Of course I am wise enough to realise I must keep my name and the association with The Den, Sodom, Yoni and Kuaidzi out of this of course. Though these are, in my opinion, excellent educational institutions not everyone would agree on that and where young, developing minds are concerned we must not be seen or thought to taint them in any way. Might get accused of bringing education into disrepute! So I have to think up a new brand and get some friends with unblemished reputations and associations as sleeping partners. It would be good to use the Oxford or Cambridge names but must be careful over intellectual property rights . . . . and anyway to be honest, those have already been used by some Chinese companies who are already set up in this line of business! So no chance of registering those names here now. Not easy to get the right name that will attract the Chinese market. Phonetic transliteration doesn't always work. Positive overtones of nobility and romance is something to aim for but that doesn't always work. For example there's a company here that called itself Windsor, thinking I guess, that that would be a name whose associations would really pull in the punters. UK royal family, Windsor Palace etc. Unfortunately, the English pronunciation of Windsor sounds too much like the Chinese name for mosquito—not a wise decision! Bit like the advert *You're never alone with a Strand* that went desperately wrong for that brand of cigarettes. Or the comment from the boss of Ratners about selling crap. You're only as good or as bad as your last advert or your statement to your clients! Remember, all publicity is good publicity is only appropriate to the unreal, glamour world of show business . . . . and even there it proves not always to be true! Oh yes, I do my business research very thoroughly, trust me! Got to start from scratch for a name I guess. Here we always also have to consider what a Chinese translation would mean—it rarely has to be literal! I also to have to think of the UK implications. So I have to put my thinking cap on . . . . Albion Academies? (AA = Alcoholics Anonymous!) Thames Tuition? (Isle of Man?) King's Colleges? Perhaps! But all maybe a bit too anglicised? Stamford Studios? (SS!) Oh, I don't know! Must get onto John Harding. I am sure he will think of something that fits the bill. And maybe, just maybe, he will agree to be one of my silent partners—not a bad choice for him and for me for that matter. Let's see how things pan out.

BILL

Hell hath no fury like a woman scorned.

You know when I reflect on that well-known phrase I reckon Will Shakespeare must have had some Anglo-Sino relationships of the feminine variety that went seriously pear-shaped.

Yes, I have a few mates still in China and a few who have left these shores (spelt with an *s* not a *w*—pay attention!) whose stories about their doomed and traumatic relationships here with Chinese women made my hair stand on end. Yes, I did say my hair! Pay attention! You see, when the expatriate male (married, engaged or unmarried) gets to China—indeed to many places in the South East Asia or the Far East generally—he finds the availability of very attractive, young women considerably more abundant than in his country of origin. There's a feeling he has arrived like Fletcher Christian and his band mutineers in a sexual paradise : one about which he has always (should I add wet?) dreamed but until now never discovered. The reasons I am sure do not have to be spelt out for you. So even the ugliest fucker (the noun is highly appropriate) can pay his money and take his choice. Oh, yes, make no mistake, these transactions are invariably of the monetary variety. Oh and good guys pay more, remember! But then, most expatriates have money in abundance as part of their business package so whilst they may be sacrificing their marriages or their engagements or their home love life they are certainly not sacrificing their mortgages, bank balances or whatever. Most of them would endorse the statement, *I spent my money on gambling, booze and women and squandered the rest.* We refer to it here in China as suffering from yellow fever or being into bamboo.

A couple of stories will give you the idea.

Poor Alan Greenaway. Bright guy, married with two, grown up teenage daughters comes over for a short-term, sixth-month contract working for British Telecom who were doing some advising to China Telecom (and they did need that advising, trust me! And thank goodness they have taken much of the advice offered.) His wife and family not coming with him, he was the classic MBA—married but available. As head design consultant he did a bit of travelling round but was largely office based with loads of office bound meetings with the China telecom management. Of course in the office he found himself surrounded by some very smart, English speaking, young and available and what's more, attractive, Chinese ladies. Did I say he was bright? Well, yes in the educated sense i.e. good degree from Edinburgh University if I recall correctly and extremely good at his job. But he was surprisingly dumb with it. I am sure he knew the saying, *Dogs don't shit on their own doorstep!* but perhaps he never really understood what it meant or what it implied to us humans until he found out the hard way.

For a while all went well. Alan settled in, got the respect of the office and the China Telecom managers and everything was progressing smoothly. So too, it seemed, in his extra-marital love life. He'd been dating (God, that sounds so passé!) Rosey, the senior office administrator and in quite a short time she had become his sleeping partner (though he referred to her as his sleeping dictionary!) and to all intents and purposes they were living full-time together. A no strings arrangement as far as he was concerned. Unfortunately, Rosey didn't see it like that. As the end of his contract drew near, naturally Rosey was getting anxious. When was he going to declare his true love for her by making his offer of marriage? After all she'd given herself to him in every which way a Chinese lady could possibly do—and that's pretty comprehensive I can assure you. She knew the office grape vine was gossiping about her so their relationship really was public knowledge and there was no way she was going to lose face. So now, it was time he told his wife at home that he'd found the new love of his life so he should be saying to her Bye, Bye Birdie, Move Over Darling and Walk away, please go . . . . And at the same time saying to Rosey, Welcome to my World, Sweet Child of mine and Hello, young lover . . . .

Of course, Alan had to give her the bad news—It's Over, Love don't live here any more etc! Sure, he wanted to, indeed he tried to let her down gently as the saying goes but Rosey was not going to let him off that easily. Although she knew about his wife and daughters and even had contact details of them she wasn't going to and didn't use that obvious route. As senior office administrator she was responsible for visas amongst other things and her first step was to blackmail him by telling him she could prevent him leaving the country if she wanted to. Alan panicked and being so scared (he clearly wasn't that bright—I'm obviously flattering him!) he did not even attempt to try to find out if she was telling the truth or not—which of course she wasn't. To cut a long story short he paid her 75,000RMB (that's 7,500 quid to you and me) to avoid that situation. That was that : or so he thought. But he forgot he was in China. Then, about a fortnight before he was due to leave she knew he had a major meeting with the hierarchy of the company in the boardroom scheduled in the morning. On the day, after the meeting had just got underway, she waltzed into the boardroom, walked up to where he was sitting and smacked him hard across the face and then laid into him screaming and shouting all the abusive Chinese phrases she could think of to denounce him as a manager, a person, a foreign devil and naturally worst of all as a really poor lover! Because of her company position she had also alerted security to her intentions and got their cooperation or should I say collaboration of course and they had alerted the police (which she had told them to do, of course) so within minutes they, the police and, of course China Telecom managers were all in the office involved in the fracas Rosey had so carefully stage managed. It really was much worse than being savaged by a dead sheep. Well, obviously it was all over for Alan. Rosey, clearly the injured party (well, in Chinese terms anyway even if not physically so!) got all the sympathy. Alan told me that when he did eventually get to passport control at the airport when he was leaving he was shitting himself just in case Rosey's long arm of the law was going to get him even though he had paid up the blackmail money. But he did get home and away though I have no idea as to how he eventually sorted things out with his family. Strangely enough, he did keep his job at BT and I did hear they'd posted him to Bangkok. Can you believe that? Maybe every cloud has a silver lining after all. Maybe he'd proved himself the right man for the Thailand assignment. So it was that Alan found that paradise, not hell, is where you are well and truly damned!

So much for Alan. Jim Erwin's story doesn't have quite such a happy ending. (Indeed, it's not over even as I write!)

Jim was a womaniser from the word go. No one was quite sure whether he was married or had been married but that really didn't matter. Brought over by Tesco's as they were linking up with Hymal to get into the Chinese supermarket business he was stationed in Shanghai but had to do a fair bit of travelling within about a 100km plus radius. Trips to Nanjing in the north and Hangzhou in the south were commonplace so he naturally met with a fair few of the locals! After about 6 months of getting to know the market both literally and metaphorically, Jim settled down with Christine, a very attractive senior buyer and top manager for Hymal and to all intents and purposes they led the life of a happy couple. Christine was a mature, sensible lady in her early thirties and fully accepted the fact that she would have Jim as a lover for the duration of his posting and that would be the end of that. During that time she would milk him for whatever she could and that would be a lot, she was sure of that! Jim was always to be seen out with her—wining and dining at the best restaurants, going to the Grand Theatre and to concerts at the Performing Arts Centre, taking short holidays out of China, attending The Britcham Ball, The Irish Ball, The Aussie Ball and the brightest and best shopping malls in

Nanjing Xi Road and Luijiahui! In all expatriates' eyes a totally recognisable and acceptable couple.

Christine's family lived in Wuxi a short distance from Shanghai and on some weekends she would go home to see them. Jim did not go with her : not really wanting the family associations and its attendant baggage that comes with any serious relationship between expatriate man and local woman. So it was that one weekend when Christine was en famille, Jim went for a drink at a local bar, Full House Two, in Hengshan Road. Although this area had a bit of a reputation, this particular bar was quite quiet and had some good live music and did not attract some of the more questionable clientele as the other bars in this strip. This Saturday evening, however, Jim noticed he was getting the come on look from a young lady who was seated further down the bar from him and who was chatting away to a guy whom Jim considered to be her Chinese boyfriend. When the boyfriend got up to go and answer the call of nature, the young lady approached Jim, gave him her mobile number and asked him straight out to phone her the next day. Such forwardness took Jim a bit by surprise but he stayed at the bar and she continued to give him the odd smile and flash of her eyes (her legs were obscured by her boyfriend standing beside her!) and the more he looked the more he found her attractive : well, sexy and sensual more than attractive he told me. Maybe it was her youth—he later found out she was only 20 : maybe it was her lithe young body : maybe it was those flashing eyes, those Jezebel, come-and-get-me smiles. But most likely it was simply just the temptation of a really good fuck with a lively young lady who was clearly up for it! Whatever, Jim got involved with Lisa as she called herself . . . . whilst still living with Christine!

For a while he managed to keep the two worlds totally separate but to believe that Christine is Christine and Lisa is Lisa and never the twain shall meet was defying all the accepted rules of engagement in Shanghai's expatriate world. So it was that Lisa found out about Christine and, being young and volatile as she was, really took up the cudgels against the poor man who had so deceived her. She went round to his apartment when fortunately (or so it seemed) Christine wasn't there, managed to get in and even managed to get him locked out of it at least for a few hours. (Jim never exactly explained to me how she managed to do this but I guess he was so afraid of this spitfire of a woman that he wasn't thinking straight and inadvertently got on the wrong side of the door!) Jim was frantic worrying about the damage she might do in the apartment on her own. He went to the reception area of the compound, they got the police but it was sometime before the termagant let him and his entourage (by now the security guard and two policemen) into the apartment. On entering Jim was somewhat relieved to see she hadn't done any damage at all. He was later to find this was not really the case! She was weeping and wailing and screaming and accusing him in Chinese of every possible crime against womanhood under the sun but mainly denouncing him as a manager, a person, a foreign devil and a really poor lover. The security guard disappeared rapidly having done his job by getting the police and getting them and Jim back into the apartment. The police looked and acted totally indifferent to the situation and Jim guessed (probably rightly) they had seen and heard something like this quite a few times before. The waited until Lisa had cried her eyes out, had her say, made herself hoarse by her shouting and screaming, made herself a dishevelled looking wreck of a woman and then conducted her away from the scene. Thus letting Jim see the havoc he had wrought on such a young, susceptible young lady. Of course, they spoke no English so could say nothing to Jim but they conveyed by their looks and action or mainly inaction that Jim had been a right prat and hopefully he wouldn't be one again for the rest of his time in China.

All gone, all quiet, Jim decided to have a more detailed check around his apartment to see if he initial observations were correct. Indeed, no visual damage had been done but when checking through the drawers in his bedroom he noticed his passport had disappeared and even more to his horror so had Christine's. Lisa! What a she-devil, what a damned clever thief she had been! This really was a body blow. He couldn't get back to the police and accuse her of stealing as she had probably by now got rid of the passports or at least would deny she knew anything about them and had hidden them away. What a pain in the arse it would be to get the passports renewed! But worse still, how could he explain the loss to Christine? Well, it was game over with Lisa for sure and possibly it was going to be game over with Christine. He decided he had to be up front with her and hoped honesty was the best policy.

Christine, you will remember, was a mature, sensible lady in her early thirties and fully accepted the fact that she would have Jim as a lover for the duration of his posting and that would be the end of that. She listened calmly to his confession and saw him for the prat he really was (and she had always thought he was). But should she play the spurned woman and walk away from the good life he had given her? Mei banfa! Oh, no! She had to use the common parlance, got him over a barrel. She wasn't the blackmailing type, at least not in the same overt sense, that Rosey was but in a much more insidious way. She knew Jim would feel so gutted he had cheated on her he would want to make things up and he would want the rest of his stay to be as calm and untroubled as possible. So relax. O.K. What's done, was done. His fate would be lingering.

Sure, he would live on with Christine and she would be a constant reminder to him of his personal failing, of his deceitfulness towards her, so he would forever have to be making it up to her. And he would certainly think twice of any future dalliance. Whenever he was with her, feeling guilty, or whenever he was apart from her, longing for her, he would have no peace. This lingering love life was made worse for Jim when Tesco was so impressed by his achievements (well those in the workplace at least as reported by the Hymal management) that they increased his posting by another three years. Lucky for Christine. (Well she was a senior buyer and top manager for Hymal!) Unlucky for Jim. To paraphrase Thomas Hardy : He carries wounds not mortal that none can cicatrize : not mortal, but lingering, worse! So it was that Jim found that redemption really lies not in heaven but in self-denial hell!

Now I am a bit of a conspiracy theorist (as you will discover if you read my one and only published novel to date that is) and in terms of this relationship I think it was a set up. Here's why. Was it coincidence that Christine was away on the weekend Lisa was in Full House 2? Christine certainly knew it was one of Jim's haunts when she was away. Did Christine know Lisa? Maybe they had crossed paths before? Not sure about that but then again, usually a spurned woman would certainly trash something in the apartment or home of the lover who has rejected or been double dealing with her. But she didn't do any damage at all—just took the passports. And how did Lisa know where the passports were? Oh, and I have heard that Hymal/Tesco are opening a branch in Luzhou, Lisa's home town, and she has been appointed as liaison manager on that project. But don't tell Jim! He's not in on the Luzhou development. Damn clever, these Chinese.

If you're an expatriate man reading these two tales of woe let them be a lesson to you. Though you may like Alan arrive at the Delectable Mountains (in his case, Thailand) you will have the most god awful time of getting there and you will certainly wonder if indeed it was all worthwhile. If like Jim you initially find variety is the spice of life you will inevitably end up with your favourite dish and for all its attraction it will eventually leave a bitter taste in your mouth. Familiarity breeds contempt!

If you are the wife, fiancée, girl-friend of an expatriate male who is given a posting out here . . . . there ain't nothing you can do about it . . . . not even should you accompany him out here. Just wait and see what happens and hope and pray that it doesn't end in tears : sorry but that's the best advice I can give.

Well, gotta go. There's someone waiting to see me . . . .

WU DABIN &
JIANG SHULIN

Things are ticking over for us. Dongdong had a good time in Beijing with her friend, LaLa. I think she was quite thrilled to visit the wonderful capital city of our great country. Certainly came back with plenty of stories and photos as she did from her UK visit. Some were quite amusing especially when she told us about seeing Chairman Mao's embalmed body in his mausoleum. She reckons his corpse is a fake! Oh, young people! I ask you! Their heads get stuffed full of nonsense and they are certainly a little more disrespectful than we were in our days but I guess we have to accept their naivety and immaturity in this respect. No doubt she'll be telling me the Long March didn't take place soon! Well, she will learn and understand more when she's older! Must say, she's a lucky girl, for sure, with all her travelling and all she's seen and done. She needs time and experience to reflect on it all though. She's now getting back into to study mode thank goodness as it is important that she gets a good Gao Kao score. I am sure she will and getting her nose to the grindstone will eliminate all these silly ideas in her head at least for the time being! Maybe hopefully for good!

I am taking time out as I said to be with her so I am hoping my husband is behaving himself in my absence in Shanghai. Not easy leaving a man in Shanghai on his own but I am sure he is o.k. He is a good man. A really good, industrious worker and a great and loyal husband. (Am I saying all that to reassure myself? I hope not!) He phones regularly and gives me all the latest news including the decline of the school at which he was previously employed. Benny, the driver keeps him suitably informed and Ms Fu keeps me suitably informed! Seems like there's been some serious financial mismanagement there by the greedy Chinese owners and this is putting the very future of the school in jeopardy. How sad. But then, some people when they get a sniff of money get carried away. Can't keep their noses out of the trough.

He has also told me that he has learned that our dear Mr Harding has changed jobs. Still in education but now working with Chinese schools and building up international courses for them. That really is wonderful news. I am sure his expertise is just what's needed by way of reforms in our educational system. It will also open up opportunities for our up and coming generation. Really good! No doubt when we next see him he will tell us all about his new line of work. Or rather he will tell Ms Fu in English and she will tell us in Chinese!

Meanwhile, I have learned that Daisy, the Marketing Manager, is pregnant! Don't know much about the circumstances but she has a new lover so the grapevine says. Seems he is Spanish and he is a regular visitor to China on business. He's in the wine trade. Don't know what he's doing selling wines to us as we have our own excellent vineyards and produce plenty of our own excellent wines. I know the foreign devils mock our home vintages with slurs like saying Die Nasty instead of Dynasty, one of our favourite and really good fermentations! Or saying that our Great Wall brand has a bouquet like a Chinese Dragon lady's breath and tastes like the water in Suzhou Creek. That's really insulting, don't you think? Totally unacceptable! I guess he's selling to the UK grocery/supermarket store developments here in the big cities like Marks and Spencer and Tesco/Hymal. Well, it will be interesting to see what produce they come up with once they open. Might sample some of what they have to offer but I bet it's not as good as our own supermarkets. I hear they do a tinned version of sweet and sour chicken and some of our other dishes like chow mein. O.K. for the expatriates I am sure but hardly good enough for our refined palates!

I guess Daisy will leave the school nearer her delivery time. That should be about 7 months hence or so. That could prove a good opportunity for me as Dongdong will have completed her Gao Kao by then and I will be back in Shanghai. She'll be wanting a full time Ayi then I reckon—the baby will need looking after! Oh and I hope Dongdong will gain a place at a university in Shanghai as having her nearby will be useful to say the least. Things are looking up for sure. Bright prospects.

Well now, isn't it good to have some gossip about Mr Harding, Mr Wu's former school and Daisy. It's gossip that makes the world go round, for sure, and it makes life out here in peasants' ville (that's what I call this particular part of the province where Mr Wu's parents live) at least just about acceptable! Thank goodness for mobile phones and the thought of getting back to Shanghai!

FU

Just been up to Beijing. Had a great time and went shopping at Xinkongtiandi, the Place and at North Sanlitun Village. Wangfujing is a bit past it now as a shopping mecca. The old order changeth, yielding place to new as the saying goes! Got to show off my education courtesy of Mr Harding—John to me—from time to time. Found this fantastic new shoe shop there—Labourtin. Oh, my God! The shoes. Lovely! Gorgeous! Yes, yes, I know expensive—over 10,000RMB but . . . . A must have. Oh, yes, a must have.

Bit concerned though about Mr Harding—John to me. He took me to Den of Iniquity—a place that lives up to its name, that's for sure. Bit of a cattle-market really but I guess an up market cattle market (if there is such a thing!) but, let's be honest, a cattle market all the same! I was surprised by his taking me there—not his kind of place for sure but he wanted to introduce me to Michelle, the owner, and he explained how he was advising her about her daughter's transfer to a school in the UK and then on to university and he was also helping her friend, Jenny, about her daughter's education as well. On top of all that, he was involved in giving advice about opening up a school in Mongolia! Hope he doesn't get any ideas about going to work there! Trust me, I'm not concerned about the place itself or the weather there, I assure you but . . . . enough said (or should I say, implied?) I am sure you get my drift.

Well, yes I met Michelle. I guess we got on OK but it takes one to know one. Know what I mean? I don't want her getting her claws into Mr Harding—John to me! I can see she's playing on his good, kind, considerate nature. So I will have to make sure my playing on his good, kind considerate nature is stronger than hers. Mind you, she's shit rich and that makes me a bit concerned but I think I have an advantage having known him and his ways for a damn sight longer than she has. Sorry, this is bringing out a bit of the worst in me, isn't it? Yes, I'm just a jealous woman : aren't we all when it comes down to it? He's my man and I'm his woman, that's all there is to say!

I met with Jenny as well when I was there. Not at The Den of Iniquity I might add. If you met her you'd know that was an impossibility. Such a prude and stuck up with it. Not a good advert for modern China, I'm telling you. She looks a bit anorexic to be honest and no matter what clothes she wears—and she has all the designer stuff, I'm telling you—they look ill-fitting and she doesn't look comfortable in them. She told me all about the Mongolian venture and I guess she's pretty switched on business wise with regard to real estate etc. Can't fault her on that score. Unlike Michelle, I don't see her as any competition for my Mr Harding—John to me—and anyway she seems interested in this Australian guy, James Parkinson, who is setting up the mining deal in Mongolia. Well, he's welcome to her, that's for sure. If he ever gets his way with her it would be like making love to a stick insect. Did not meet him but she told me all about him. I did meet her daughter—another anorexic piece of work and not very communicative but I guess that's typical of teenagers. Can't say I was the most loquacious at that age. Made up for it since though!

I also met with Peter. What can I say? Another one who is not a good advert for modern China, I'm telling you. He's a born loser though he likes to think he's a mover and a shaker. Oh, and his big, fat five plus bellies minder! Apart from his bellies he had bigger tits than many of my girl friends. Ugh! What can I say? Not a good advert for modern China, I'm telling you. It's a wonder he manages to sit in the driving seat of that Mercedes. Doesn't need an air bag in the event of an accident. In Newtonian terms (forces—action/reaction—know what I mean?) his rolls of fat would save him from serious injury that's for sure. Come to think of it, perhaps he would disprove the laws of exchange of momentum in collision! Well, it's the exception that proves the rule, isn't it?

We also visited some of the local hostelries. The Goose and Duck was a bit of a dive but the owner, Frank was pleasant enough. The Rickshaw was also a bit crummy and quite stiflingly hot and everything seemed to revolve around the pool table! But the Pavilion was very tasteful indeed. Very much up to Shanghai standards if I may say so. We also went to the Den Bar to watch some football. It's very pleasant and welcoming but Mr Harding—John to me—seemed to be on more than good terms with all the ladies (young girls) that served there. We also met some of his rugby playing friends there. A really good crowd and great atmosphere I have to admit so it's easy to see why he likes this place. My favourite, he said.

So overall I, (or should I say we?) had a good time but on one occasion I did press one of the wrong buttons on Mr Harding—John to me. Indeed, I set off one of his purple patches—shouldn't that be rages? . . . . must tell Mr Wu—and that was a bit scary. I only mentioned that I would like to have little dog but I'd hardly said just that when he exploded!

When I first came to China in 1996, he shouted, *any dog (or come to that cat) you saw would definitely be called Lucky. Now these animals, especially the dogs, have become a fashion statement. Horrible little runts of animals some no bigger than rats, sometimes with their fur dyed to match their owner's accessories, or sometimes kitted out in their own clothes to complement their owners get up!* Owned by people who live in high rises and who work all day, these creatures hardly get any exercise. *What their apartments must smell like give their excrement or piss I hate to think. I suppose,* he rounded on me, *you were going to say you want one because it would be a companion for you. Well who is going to be a companion for it when we are together here or on holiday? And who's going to pay for such inconvenience? Can't think that kennels come cheap in China! Wow, that must be a growth business!* He paused. *Finally,* he continued, *if this trend continues,* he claimed, *then we would not walk through China's cities getting our shoes covered with spittle and snot by the people gobbing off but through piles of dog shit. It's already happening! What is China going to do about it?* I took all that for a no and let the matter drop.

So ended quite a social visit to the capital as well as the usual shopping one. Didn't get those shoes though. However, it's only a matter of time!

BILL

I did say from the off that I love China. And, for sure, I really do. However, there are a few things China needs to address before it can be taken seriously by the rest of the world.

There's the ticket touts or scalpers as they are referred to here. For every and each event they buy up heaps of lower priced tickets in advance thus in the first instance pushing the ticket cost for the laowai (foreigner) coming to purchase tickets into the middle and higher price range. Then on the evening of the play, concert, gig or whatever they are hanging around and trying to persuade you to buy tickets even though they are well aware if you have got tickets, you have got yours legally. Of course, they always pick up some customers and occasionally I have heard of someone getting a bargain deal. But it's always these exceptions you hear about—rarely if ever the details of those who got duly ripped off. On the other hand I have known expats pay exorbitant prices and on occasions actually seen some sad cases who have been duped and their fake purchases get them turned away from the venue. There's always a market for tickets like this but how about doing it (if it has to be done at all and I guess it has—well that's the way it now works in the UK) through the internet? Far preferable and keeps these scum away—or at least makes them faceless . . . . one of the beauties of the internet!

While we are on the subject of concerts etc. it has taken quite a few years to get the Chinese audience to accept that you do not clap between movements during a classical symphony, concerto or whatever. A real victory that. However, there is one more step that needs to be taken but it needs the cooperation of the visiting orchestras, ensembles etc. It is heart-warming that the Chinese love to attend concerts and they really do appreciate their music. It is also good of them to applaud loud and long some of the thrilling performances they hear . . . . but they are reluctant to accept a concert programme is a concert programme—job done, so they have this expectation of encores. Regretably, visiting musicians have entered into this conspiracy : thus the programme has ended with the sonourous dying strains of Tchaikovsky's Pathetique symphony. What is needed is applause and a chance to leave and reflect on the cathartic experience such music has given to the audience. But . . . . no, let's give them an encore. Well, they could have chosen one of Beecham's Lollipops as he referred to what he considered interesting but slight masterpieces by say Delius, Elgar, Holst, Britten or, if desperate, even Finzi! No, those are considered not appropriate. Star Wars Film Music—that's the ticket to send everyone off. To be honest, it's very hard to recall the subtleties of Tchaikovsky after such a fortissimo splurge of brashness. I could give other examples. It's going to be a long haul but maybe we can win this one as well. By way of analogy, would an acting company do a reprise of something like The Green Eye of the Yellow God as an extra tidbit after a performance of King Lear or Oedipus Rex? I don't fucking well think so!

Then there's spitting. Well, it's not so much spitting as, although that still occurs, it's not as prevalent as it was. But the sucking in of phlegm, snot and all internal throat spittle/liquid remains. Hearing what sounds like some vacuum suction pump having start up difficulties is bad enough but to the sensitive Westener (that's all of us as far as I am concerned) it brings the most appalling images into one's mind. Most of whatever it is that is semi-congealed in the throat and nostrils gets sucked in and swallowed so what this semi viscuous conglomeration does to the stomach and how it passes though other of the body's internal organs is something that both seriously defies and distresses the imagination.

b) Spit into a piece of waste paper, then put it into a garbage can.

c) Spit on the floor of the vehicle . . . . in its driving licence written/computerised test? I promise you this is genuine!

Got to add smoking. Enough said!

And public toilets! More than enough said.

JENNY JING

Well, have I got a big smile on my face? Yes, of course I have. Why? Well, James and I are an item. He's over here quite a bit of course, virtually permanently now since the mining is really taking off in Mongolia. We certainly enjoy each other's company and have had some good times together. I really feel like a teenager in love nowadays. Really! I haven't let him go all the way yet, of course. Oh no! That would be a bit too much too soon. No, we're not intimate yet, but . . . . However, Michelle reckons I really should get on with it! *Make no mistake, the way to a man's heart is through your vagina*, she says. Makes me blush to think of it but maybe she's right. I guess it's only a matter of time.

Lala seems OK about things. That's good. We know how temperamental teenagers can be about these things, don't we? Since I will be pretty occupied in Mongolia for a while and, since James will be up there as well, I think I will send her for another summer at The Camera School of English in Cambridge. I have talked about this with her and again she seems quite happy with that. Got to detach her from mother's apron strings. She's got to fly solo sometime. The corollary is true as well, of course. Ah, mothers and daughters! Why has no one written a novel with that title? After all we have *Fathers and Sons, Sons and Lovers, All My Sons, Sons and Daughters* . . . . sorry, I digress.

Yes, it truly is the best of times. Things are going well with the real estate work. There are now quite a contingency of workers on site and we've got them well accommodated and, of course, this has meant an influx of service industries, with attendant employees and Mongolia has had to up its facilities, supermarkets, hotels, restaurants etc in oh so many ways. I am happy to be of service on the real estate side, of course. And Michelle is happy to be involved also, of course. Her side of the entertainment business is thriving as we always knew it would be. Peter is still totally tied up with capital outlay and I must say James has well and truly got his measure! It is really interesting the stories he tells me about Peter at school in Oz. He reckons he was only not expelled because his dad kept pouring money into the school to keep him there. Reckons his dad must have funded the school library extension not to mention a new building comprising a school theatre and state of the art drama, music and arts facilities! Money talks for sure! Well, I am sure the money was not wasted on the school but it most certainly was on Peter.

Two stories I simply must tell you that James recounted about Peter which really shows how he has not changed one iota. One evening he had got out of school and gone binge drinking comme d'habitude and came back to find the huge iron front gates of the school drive closed. In his inebriated state he decided he could climb over them. He did alright until he got to the top and tried to swing over to the other side. He actually did manage to get to the other side but not by climbing down but by falling down and, of course injuring himself in the process so he couldn't get up. His moans alerted security who alerted an ambulance which when it drove up to the gates, the driver stopped, calmly got out and pushed them open and then attended along with his colleague to the forlorn, wounded student. It would have been good to see Peter's expression when the paramedic just pushed open those gates, wouldn't it?

On another inebriate night out with a couple of friends they got back to the school and decided to play cards in the recreation room on the second floor of the school main building. All three were pretty pissed, as they say, and had been sick out of the window onto the ground below. Peter, having as usual drunk too much, needed to relieve himself but could not be bothered to go along the corridor to the lavatory. Instead, he sat on the window ledge and proceeded to unbutton his fly and as if almost in slow motion, slid off the ledge onto the ground below, once again seriously injuring himself—this time breaking both legs. His screams shocked his confederates into sobriety so they called an ambulance and alerted security. When the ambulance arrived, his comrades in debauchery looked down on the scene from the window and heard the paramedics remark, *Poor chap. He's been in such pain he's been sick and wet himself.* Plus ca change, plus ca la meme chose, as they say. Sounds like Peter spent as much time in hospitals as he did in school! Interestingly enough as James explained nearly all stories about Peter involved drinking. He boasted about his sexual exploits but none of these could ever be verified. Certainly boys have a habit of saying they've had it when they haven't and girls saying they haven't when they've had! A saying not without an element of truth, that's for sure. Well in quite a lot of instances so I am led to believe.

Mind you, Peter's history at school shows what money can do and I must say I am a bit envious and wish I had sufficient funds to afford to twist a few arms to get Lala into Lancing. Well, never mind all that. She will do OK and soon be able to get off and study in the UK full time.

By the way, I have actually talked James into investing in a property in Beijing. He knows it makes sense. Nice two-bedroomed apartment just down from Sanlitun Village in a brand new development down there. I got him a very good deal and he's pretty pleased with it.

Helps cement our relationship! Gives him a good place to relax at weekends and sometimes he stays and works from Beijing as well. I have provided the womanly touch so necessary to these bachelor pads and I think he likes that. Maybe I'll spend sometime time with him there in the near future. Who knows? Nudge nudge, wink, wink! I do keep thinking of what Michelle has said . . . . and she has proved right in the past! It really is just a matter of time!

Meanwhile, Mr Harding has proved to be very helpful indeed about setting up a school. He did a detailed business plan and also had several suggestions as to design of buildings, layout etc. Quite a costly business but a good investment for any developer and we've got Peter on to that, naturally! However, Mr Harding came down a bit in my estimation somewhat when he introduced me to Fu Langong, whom he said was his P.A. P.A.? Comfort woman more like! I can tell a mile off. Can't fool me! Mind you she was quite pleasant and had real style in her dress sense and had some really beautiful clothes and accessories . . . . courtesy of Mr Harding I don't doubt! Could have shown Dongdong a few things! Well she knew how to conduct herself, that's for sure but she's the kind of young lady that should be behind the counter in Guggi, Ferragamo, Tod's, Prada or wherever, certainly not in front! It will all end in tears no doubt for one fine day Mr Harding will have to vacate our country and head back whence he came—sad for him, sadder for her!

Oh, finally, Lala has asked me if she can have a dog. Well, I can't deny her that can I? It's very fashionable nowadays and we must keep up appearances. She's a very sensible girl and a lovely, lovely daughter. Who could ask for better? I'll take her out on the weekend and we'll see if there's something out there she is really going to like. I'm sure we'll find something—no expense spared!

PETER

Well I must say this time the shit really has hit the fan in more ways than one! Big fucking deal! I kid you not.

The old man popped his clogs just over a week ago. Very sad indeed, but it was, to be honest, not unexpected. He never had recovered in any way from his last relapse. I was really sorry he never was able to see the great deal I was doing with regard to the mineral mining in Mongolia. I really think it would have made him very proud of me. The funeral was a big occasion given all his government connections and the funeral oration was in fact given by the vice-mayor of Beijing. Impressive, eh? Quite a tribute. Loads of fucking guanxi!!!

I decided no expense should be spared and so gave him the latest for funeral send offs i.e. "taste of modernity" bits and pieces. Yeah. It's the latest to try to give the olds a sense of what the modern China is really like. I know Dad experienced some of the 21st century China in his time here but I thought it would be a nice gesture, all the same.

And anyway, his heart and mind were in the past which he referred to as the good old days when cadres did their jobs in accordance with Chairman Mao's instructions and people lived a happy life without worry and anxiety. I mean, "As if!" So along with the paper money for burning I also got replicas of iPhones, ipads, a Ferrari, some Gucci shoes and suits and a super villa (not Neuschwanstein I might add) but all very tasteful and top of the range replicas, naturally! I drew the line at bikini clad mistresses! Yes, you can get those, sure enough! Oh, I'm sure Dad had a few in his time (and not necessarily bikini clad!) but I didn't want to give offense and personally I don't think that's very tasteful! At times there's a tendency to go OTT on things, I think! Come to think of it, perhaps I was really thinking of myself when I eventually kick the bucket. There'd be no room for me in my coffin if my friends or relations got those for me (bikini clad or otherwise!)

There was a very good turn out. Jenny and Michelle both made it as I expected and even James came along which was very good of him as he obviously never ever knew my father. They were all very impressed by the Vice Mayor's valedictory and Michelle for sure congratulated him on it. Nandia and Anna also came which I thought was very sweet of them. They helped me keep my pecker up on what was such a solemn occasion. So nice to have the support of such good friends. Mum came back from

Moscow and two of her new Russian friends came with her. I asked about Ivan and Igor and she said they were doing well and apologized for not being able to come but business commitments at present were pretty demanding. They were now focusing on the Olympics in London believe it or not! Very entrepreneurial! Since Nadia and Anna were there I thought it wise not to ask about Yana.

Perhaps I am a bit sensitive but I felt I got some nasty stares from some of the cadres who were present. Kind of evil eye stuff. Can't think why. It wasn't as if I'd murdered my old man or anything! We held a reception after the cremation in our palatial mansion, Neuschwanstein, but not everyone came back for that. Not even the Vice-Mayor. Said he had important business that couldn't wait. Well, he is a big shot after all! A bit of a disappointment there. But to be honest it wasn't very satisfactory as some of the few remaining bottles of wine we brought up from the cellars were decidedly off! (There was some left over vodka from the Olympic days but I didn't think that was appropriate for an after Dad's funeral bash. He was Chinese after all! Bai Jiu would have been far more appropriate. However, I've made a mental note that we must get the storage of wine in the cellars properly dealt with.) Before Mum left, her Russian friends gave me a bill for use of the mansion for the after-funeral reception. I couldn't figure this out so I asked Mum about it. "Just part of the deal. Remember?" she said.

"What deal was that?" I asked.

"Oh, you remember when you got the money for the mineral mining business. All those papers you signed. Got to give something back to those who helped you then," she said. All a bit vague if you ask me. To be honest I am not sure what she was on about but she asked me to pay a.s.a.p. so as she said, there'd be no trouble! Peculiar that—what trouble could there possibly be? Certainly all a mystery to me but I paid up and off she went with her comrades! She said she would be in touch but I haven't heard from her since she left to go back.

Well, anyway, here I am just trying to get to grips with Dad's demise and sorting out all the financial and legal entanglements thereto—and, boy, are there plenty of those!—when my minder comes in and thrusts a copy of a local newspaper in front of me and what do I read as a major headline?

Unlicensed Mining Firm faces Big Fine!

Bloody hell! I must confess my hands were shaking as I clutched the newspaper and read on . . . .

A Mining Company in Ulaanbaatar has been fined more than 727 million yuan (US$115,000,000) for continuing to operate while applying for a licence though having been advised from the outset that this was illegal. The fine was imposed by The Land and Resources Bureau in Inner Mongolia on a Joint-Venture Australian Company and it could be higher *still. Bureau officials have stated the fine could rise to over 1 billion yuan to punish the company for additional illegal profits. The company has around 2,000 employees and the management and finances of the company are now subject to further intensive investigations which are currently on-going. There has, said a spokesman, clearly been a violation of legal procedures and it is important that a thorough investigation into the company, its management and its financial practices are carried out.*

You can imagine what this has done to my heart rate! I have tried phoning James but there's no response there. So I tried Jenny. She said she hadn't heard from James for a couple of days and she also had difficulty trying to get hold of him. She promised to get back in touch if she had any more news. She seemed quite calm as she told me yes, she had read the news and just advised me not to get over-excited about things. Michelle was not much help either. She said she had little to do with James but dealt more directly with the work force and as far as she was concerned everything was going well. She also told me not to worry : things could always be worked out. "Right money in the right places is what's required," she reminded me. "After all this is China! Everything is possible."

Maybe she's right but that doesn't help my heart palpitations at present!

Now, just when I think I am at my wits' end in trying to get to the bottom of all of this I notice a couple of police cars, lights blazing and sirens sounding have just pulled up outside! What the fuck are they doing here? As if I had not enough things to think about. Better go and see what they want I suppose! I haven't been speeding or doing any drink driving of late so God knows why they are here this time . . . . If my minder has been up to anything in my cars then his days are numbered!

"Yes, officer, how can I help you . . . ."

MICHELLE

"Man's life is a cheat and a disappointment." So wrote the poet. You can find out who if you get on to www.google.co.uk! Well maybe for some that is. For men? Ah yes, well maybe! They deserve it! And it won't be long until you'll see it applies to some person or persons I (and you by now) know. However, definitely not to me. Mei banfa!

Oh, sure the Mining Company has had to shell out a fucking small fortune i.e. seriously it is a fucking small fortune to them as you can well imagine, but believe me, Hu Jintao's in Zhongnanhai and all's well in the Chinese world (at the time of writing this that is!) And even with the change of government, politburo or whatever later this year it will still be OK, trust me! Right money in the right places at the right time is what was needed and sadly James and Peter didn't quite get that right from the off. Their funeral! No good crying over spilt milk as they say! Never mind, not to worry. The business (under mainly Chinese new management now naturally .... and thriving, of course) is still fully operational in Mongolia and so for me nothing has changed. Well, it has actually because now it is employing even more workers than before so my business is booming.

I now already have one large restaurant here, three bars and a fucking (yes, I feel that adjective is highly appropriate) huge night club. The restaurant is called Lost Heaven because, to be honest, the food you get in this part of the world is pretty shit and so it reminds (or should remind) the workers of what they are missing out on. Strangely enough, they seem to enjoy the fare and are willing to pay good prices for the sheep (yes, sheep i.e. mutton, definitely not lamb! Mutton dressed as mutton—no frills!), goat meat with occasional camel and horsemeat thrown in so that's fine by me. Well, flavor it all with chilli and who knows the difference? What a fucking joke! No one is daft enough to drink the camel and goat milk of course but we do use those in cooking. No good trying to sell smoothies here! The bars? Well there's a mixture of locals, Han Chinese and mainly Aussies here so I have named them Kylie's Watering Hole, Hong Shin (Red Star to you!) and Khan Khan Bar. I am sure you can guess the clientelle appropriate to each one, though to be honest they're all pretty ram jam packed most nights of the week. Got the right balance of imported beers (no problems thanks to the new Chinese management) to go round so we keep the customers satisfied for sure. The night club—it's fucking (yes, I feel that adjective is highly appropriate) huge as it has to accommodate 1,000+ most nights and that certainly does not include the entertainment staff!—is called City of Ulaanbaatar Nightly Treats. We have a strict membership scheme and designate certain nights to certain members otherwise we'd be more than oversubscribed or should I say the entertainment staff would be—well maybe not over-subscribed is right but over something—I am sure you can fill in the missing word! Got to smile because I have just thought not only would they be fucked but they would also be fucked! Get it? The English language has such excellent puns! However, the local government didn't want anything with overt sexual implications such as Sodom and Gomorrah and Den of Iniquity (very reserved of them for sure!) and they insisted I had to identify the city in the title. I think I got it just about right to satisfy them . . . . and the clientele (and me, or course), don't you? The main initials look great in 1 metre neon lights at the club's entrance. Visible over many a long mile! Eat your heart out, Las Vegas. So as the miners mine the minerals (there's some grand canyons in this part of the world, fellahs, believe me!) and the beer slurps, slurps, slurps down their gullets and they cream, cream, cream their pants every so often (probably more often than I care to think about), my God how the money rolls in! Naturally, the new management is entitled to its cut and so we are all very satisfied. A win-win situation, don't you think?

It's livened up this part of the world that's for sure. It's also helped the Beijing economy as now many of the Mongolian molls are happy to have found useful employment here and so they don't migrate back and forth to Beijing. (To plagiarize Bob Dylan, They don't have to work in Maggie's bar no more—that's an in joke for Beijingers and expatriates who know the city : other readers will have to work it out. Well, it's not difficult!) In turn, the Beijing broads are happier now that they have more opportunities (and much less serious competition than before!) so they feel much more secure on their home turf. Another win-win situation, don't you think? Got to think of the good of the nation as a whole! What was it your philosopher said? Greatest happiness of the greatest number! Well, we try. Mind you, let's say all Chinese are happy but some are more happy than others! A lot more happy indeed!

It's the way of the world, isn't it! Talking of which I've gone from China to Mongolia. Should I go global? Tomorrow the world? First we take Manhattan . . . . Early days yet, I think. No need to expand or diversify too quickly.

Mr Harding has been very helpful both to me and Jenny. He's certainly ensured a place for my daughter at a good university in the UK. Must say he's a charming man. A real gentleman. Well educated and quite a catch. It would be good if he could stay in Beijing for a while that's for sure but I am not sure exactly what his future plans are. There was talk of him either going south to Guangzhou which has the highest crime rate in China and whose stifling climate serves as a sauna, or north-west to Xi'An, which masquerades as a city of culture since it's home to the terracotta warriors. But beneath its cultural exterior it is decidedly unsophisticated and pretty dirty in the true dirt sense of the word. Well, it's has a lot of the population who are Moslems, hasn't it? Sorry if that sounds politically incorrect but it is politically incorrect, I know. I really don't think he would like either of those two venues. I'll see if I can persuade him otherwise. Founding Principal of the new school in Ulaanbaatar—certainly not too attractive I know, but maybe I can show him it's got some built in advantages? Additional attractions, so to speak! Nudge, nudge, wink, wink . . . . know what I mean? Where there's a will, there's a way!

JENNY JING

It was the best of times; it was the worst of times. Who the Dickens wrote that? Doesn't matter! Well, it really is a bitter sweet time for me. To be honest I don't know whether to laugh or cry. So which part of the news do you want first? The good news or the bad news? (This is not the start of a joke, believe me.) Let's start with the bad. Get it over and done with.

James. He's gone. Gone! Out of my life forever . . . . unless I decide to go and see him in Australia and I don't really fancy that of course. Just after he and I were getting it together. Or should I say getting it on together? Oh yes, I took Michelle's advice and I am glad I did. But now? Well it's over and done with and that makes me feel a bit bitter. Without a man again. Story of my life. Of course, he was entangled in all the problems with the mining company and rather than prosecute him—well we don't want to have inharmonious relations with our Asian neighbours, the Australians, now, do we?—the powers that be decided it was best he went home, his visa revoked never ever to be renewed. As Michelle would no doubt say : end of fucking story! (Literally and metaphorically in my case obviously!) Well at least he didn't have time to prove himself unfaithful like the two other men in my life. It was odd though that he once said to me it is possible to love someone and still be unfaithful to them. Well, that sums up men, doesn't it? And he whispered in my ear, *Faith unfaithful kept him falsely true*, which he said applied to Lancelot in the Camelot story. Frankly I hadn't a clue what he was talking about and now I don't really care. Michelle says forget it and forget him and move on. But it sticks in my mind and makes me think there's no way you can trust men even when they seem as nice as James really was. Are they all bastards? I guess it was only a matter of time!

Maybe! Maybe not! So, onto the good news. There's two parts to this!

Some good can come of men . . . . occasionally. You may recall that I managed to get James to buy an apartment in Beijing. Well, now of course it's no use to him and he can't really claim it being out of the country and no longer entitled to a visa and be resident here. Of course, I have contacted him and told him how sad I am that this has happened. I have promised to re-sell it but explained the problems with that. Well, prices have dipped seriously, of course, so there's no way he's going to get all his money back : no, not even at the low price I managed to get for him when he bought it. Then, of course, selling so soon involves taxes and finally getting money out of China has become more costly and more difficult than ever. Actually, I think some of Michelle's deviousness has brushed off on me. I am not going to sell it. I am going to let it out and that will give me a nice steady—extra!—income. I will play James along. Problems in selling. Defect in the building when it was surveyed. Needs some supportive reconstruction in case of earthquakes. (That's very common nowadays after what happened in 2008 of course!) Bad market. Going to take time. So sorry. Maybe it's a bit tough on him as he was pretty good to me but maybe I am taking out my revenge on men on him. Well, tough shit. Wow, Michelle's attitude really is catching, isn't it?

And Part 2 of the good news? The Mongolian project, of course, carries on . . . . under new (Chinese) management of course. Going great guns, indeed! So my business in real estate and the development of the international school are both progressing really well. As I said previously, Mr Harding has proved very, very good in helping with the school. I know Michelle was wanting to try to talk him into becoming the founding principal but so far he has declined. I have heard, but it's probably only rumours, that she's tried (and is trying maybe?) her own female charms and wiles on him. Can't see him falling for that because it seems to me he's far too attached to his

PETER

H i! I'm writing this bit for you from prison. I expect
you've already guessed that I'd end up here. Life
inside is, as Evelyn Waugh, one of your fine authors wrote
in *Decline and Fall*, not unlike being a student in a public
school. (Didn't think I was bright enough to know that
sort of thing, did you? But I've now got time to catch up
on all that reading I never did at school! And, I must say,
it's really quite enjoyable! But, not as enjoyable as . . . . you
know what, I must confess). Being here reminds me of the
times I was gated (i.e. confined to barracks in the military
sense!) in my school in Oz. That was quite frequently given
all the shenanigans I got up to there. Yeah, I used to go out
and get trashed on 4X and Fosters and the odd spiff and
what not and, of course, there were the women. Ah those
Aussie Shielas! It's a country with a sporting culture that's
for sure and sex must be one of its top sports—though
usually all you ever hear about is cricket and Aussie rules!
Yeah I miss the sun-tanned Shielas, that's for sure. Don't
get me wrong, I miss the Mongolian and Chinese bints as

well, of course. Got to admit that's the really toughest side of being in prison. To put it bluntly, you've got to play solo while you're in here .... unless you want to get like some and become a pooftah! Not for me! Mei banfa!

So why am I banged up? Hmmm .... sometimes I sigh and ask myself that given that it seems all a set of misunderstandings really over the mineral mining contract and the deals with the Russians over the family estate before and after Dad died. You know you do everything right and no one remembers : you do one thing wrong and they never forget! Well maybe two or more things wrong in my case, to be honest! That being the situation, they threw the book at me in court but I did the right thing Chinese-wise. Admitted my guilt and showed due contrition. They like to see that. Well, truth to tell, all the indictments as they called them were really a bit mystifying to me. Hadn't a clue I had so transgressed the law in the ways they said but I suppose they were right and I was wrong. Well they were lawyers, weren't they? Verdict : guilty as charged. What else? So they gave me a suspended death sentence. Sounds harsh, doesn't it? Oh no, not really. You see, being the son of an important cadre with all the right government connections—loads of fucking guanxi!—means that in 3 years' time or so, once everything has blown over I will be released and that's that! Yeah, that's the way it works here, I promise you. It's only the dregs of society, the druggies, the dealers, the child molesters, the fat cat embezzlers and pond life like that end up getting a bullet in the back of the head in the local stadium in the early hours of some weekday morning. You read in the press about loads of top guys, VIPs, on corruption charges just like me getting these suspended death sentences. Sometimes, they appeal and the death part of the sentence is removed but that's not in their favour 'cause they have then to serve about 10-15 years. But if you just bide your time, take the guilt rap, all's well and, as I say, it's an early and quiet release. So I am not appealing. I will just sit it out. Doing time, as they say and sure enough, that's what I'm doing. Or is time doing me? Oh, forget such philosophical crap! I'm not into that!

Life here is not so bad. 3 meals a day and, of course, Mum manages to get things sent in to me so I live quite well. Yeah, I get plenty of tinnies and fags . . . . and the odd spiff of course! Actually Michelle has proved to be a trooper as well as she's kept me supplied with goodies though not the usual female brand I am used to but good all the same. I also pay regular protection money to the boss here—big fucking guy, more than twice the size of my minder would you believe, and serving life for murder, rape, extortion . . . . you name it, he's done it (and is still doing it inside!) He's ex-military : gained more medals than Goering, so they say. Oh, and he's a party member! So got to keep on the right side of him for sure! Anyway, he and his gang keep me safe from the gays here thank goodness : yes, you probably have guessed, and I readily admit, I am a bit of a homophobic! Uggh! Makes me shudder just to think of those poofs. Sorry if that sounds politically incorrect but it is politically incorrect. I have also asked Nandia and Anna not to come and visit me thought they were keen to do so and did make a couple of visits early on. It's hard enough being banged up and seeing them makes things harder—both literally and metaphorically—I am sure you know what I mean. Anyway, Mum says that once I am out I can go and live in Moscow with her and her new friends so there's going to be more opportunities with the bits of skirt there eventually. I'm sure they are as good a Yana so that's something to look forward to.

James? Ah, James. Well, he fucked off back to Oz didn't he? Typical nerd. I always knew he was! Didn't I say so from the very start? When the going gets tough the nerd backs out! If you can't stand the heat, get out of the kitchen so they say and he clearly couldn't stand the heat. I guess it was not entirely his fault. They did take away his visa and, from what I hear, have banned him from ever coming back. I doubt if he minds really. And good riddance as far as I'm concerned to be honest. He was knocking off Jenny. He could have done much better than that. Christ, I could have fixed him up with any amount of women. Can't imagine what it's like making love to her. I would imagine it's the equivalent of just masterbating into a woman—no real sexual pleasure there. I bet she can't even fake an orgasm. It will be Jenny-come-quickly with her and she'll head as quickly as possible to the shower to clean herself up as she probably finds the whole thing pretty disgusting. Pathetic! Well, he's better off out of that, that's for sure. He did, though, write me a letter from Oz saying how sorry he was things hadn't worked out quite as we had hoped. He said how sad he was to hear about my court case and subsequent incarceration. He'd got the news from Jenny who he said was endeavouring to sell the apartment he had bought in Beijing. He went on to say I would be welcome to visit him in Oz after I'd done my time. Kind of him, don't you think? Still doesn't compensate for his being a nerd though. Not in my book anyway. Anyway, I doubt they'd let a convicted Chinese criminal into Oz? Or maybe not. It used to be where all the Limey convicts were sent back in the old days, wasn't it? Hope for me yet! They might welcome me with open arms! Maybe James can fix me up with some business opportunities? As if . . . .!

The family estate business is interesting. The Chinese authorities were pissed off I had (totally inadvertently and unknowingly in my opinion, though they didn't believe that in court!) signed over such an important and large piece of real estate in Beijing to the Russians. Especially so since the castle was used for important local government meetings, cadre training etc and now the Russians were charging them for the privilege. (They didn't seem to care about the use of the place for weddings—that was always quite a money spinner for us but then that wasn't spending government money, was it?) Well, it has given them something to meet and debate about and to try to work out an agreement at a fairly low governmental level. That, as it turns out is a good thing. Why? Well, the western press loves to hype up disputes between China and its neighbours and they will make a field day of this. The headlines will be indicating something like, Russia and China in land dispute in the capital Beijing—in journalese of course—*Beijing Moscow Contretemps* in The Times? *No Trespassing Beijing tells Moscow* in the tabloids? *Chinks say Fuck off Ruskies, get out of our back yard* in The Star? But we all know it's small beer in terms of our politics with Russia and therefore the big meaningful stuff at top level can go on unreported. By this method China can consolidate its dealings with Russia (and in the light of other disputes with its other neighbours) and everyone's happy—except the westerners of course who haven't yet worked out the inscrutability of the Chinese psyche.

You know, your media really is so often off target it's a joke. Every so often you come up with a story beginning with "the famous Chinese dissident" phrase about someone and we all ask, Who the fuck are you talking about? Famous to you, maybe, totally unknown to us. It's all your own hype. I think you forget we have a population of 1.3 billion and a massive land area in which we live. How many famous people are there in China?

My minder, bless him, came to see me when I was first banged up. They didn't take my cars away so he's kindly looking after those until I get out. It's been quite a while now since I have seen him though. Can't exactly call him a frequent visitor! Come to think of it, it was the last time I saw Nandia and Anna and told them not to come and visit. He had brought them to see me which was kind of him. The prison is a bit out of the city and getting here and back would have cost them a fair bit of time not to mention quite hefty taxi fares.

WU DABIN &
JIANG SHULIN

Well, we have heard the good news. Yes, Mr Harding is returning to Shanghai. Oh joy, Oh rapture unconfined! Got a top educational job from what we hear but I guess Ms Fu will tell you all about that.

Things are OK with me too. Dongdong has got her place at Shanghai Normal University where she is studying to become a teacher. She works at Carrefour part-time which helps with her funding and with the family budget! Mr Harding has also promised to make some arrangements for her to go again to the UK but this time to get a short work placement in a school there. What an opportunity! That will do her the world of good! Oh, he is such a kind, considerate man! We really are overjoyed he's coming back to this great city.

And yes, Daisy has had a lovely baby girl! Oh, she's so cute! How do I know? Well, I am her ayi/nursemaid . . . . full time! Not a wet nurse I would add! Just as nanny as you would call it. Things just couldn't have worked out better! Only downside is it's full time and I can't do any work for Mr Harding even though I wish I could. However, I have got him a friend of mine who is also a good ayi so I know he will be well looked after. Fu does that as well of course—after her fashion!

Only got Gary to worry about now but that's a little bit in the future I am pleased to say and Mr Wu has to play (and indeed is playing I can relate) his part in getting him up to scratch! Men do have their uses . . . . occasionally!

Mr Wu? Well . . . .

Hi, yes all's well with me. Actually went out to dinner with Mr Harding and some current and former colleagues just a couple of nights ago. He was down here on business. Won't be taking up his new post until August but he did say he was actively engaged in other work right now. We went to a Korean restaurant this time. It was very good—lots of beef! Plenty of Tsingdao beer as well—for sure, Mr H (I feel I'm close enough to him to refer to him that way now!) loves his beer and we love it too. Far preferable to baijiu. My better half couldn't make it now that she's got her hands full with her now job looking after Cordelia—that's the baby's name. He was in good form and was telling us about Beijing and some of the work he'd done for an international school in Mongolia where, he said, it was all happening now! Well, it's always all happening wherever you go in China, isn't it? We did tell him we'd heard about the Mining Company there which had got into trouble over licences and he said he knew a lot of those involved so he gave us a real insider's account. Not quite straight from the horse's mouth but close enough! All very interesting.

My new school has promoted me partly because they've extended their campus and also they now have a boarding house for students. More responsibility and certainly more money. We're gradually climbing up the social ladder—daughter at university and all that to boot! Might have to think about turning in our motorcycles and getting a car! Got to be cautious though. Mustn't get into those western, Eurozone habits of live now, pay later!

On the sad side, and Mr H knows all about this, his old school is being flushed down the toilet as they say thanks largely to gross financial mismanagement (embezzlement, let it be said, in some aspects of their dealing) on the part of the owners—pure greed of course—and they are aided and abetted by a new, dragon lady principal they appointed who out-Harpies the Harpies—even in looks I might add! We have a saying in the East, "can't afford to lose face." Well, she could well afford to lose hers, I'm telling you. And I don't mean metaphorically. What a monster! She's universally loathed by students, staff and parents alike even though she, herself, thinks she's the bees' knees. What is it your poet wrote : " . . . . Tae see oursel's as ithers see us?" She needs to take a good look at herself in the mirror (though it might crack if she did, I guess) and in her own mind (one has to wonder if she's got one!) and seriously consider that very wise statement. Incredible though it seems, it really is harder to make an international school fail here than by prudence to keep it open and making a profit. Says something for the management of that place after Mr H left, doesn't it? What a shower of shit the owners and management have proved to be. We're really upset about this, of course, and as Mr H said, he and the great work force (we count in amongst that lot!) who helped build and shape the school have been betrayed by selfish owners and arrogant management. Gutted was the word he used when he told us how he felt. I feel sorry for him.

On a different note, I occasionally have Gary working with me now if I am on duty on weekends or in the evenings and when he's on school vacation. Yes, he too, is back living with us now and goes to a nearby local school. Can't see him making the grade for university but he can obtain gainful employment like I have. So this is a kind of apprenticeship for him. What's better than to learn from someone like me who is a trained electrician, plumber, builder, surveyor, gas-fitter, painter and decorator, IT and telephone engineer, qualified driver (HGV and PSV), carpenter, cabinet maker, metalworker, car mechanic, swimming pool maintenance manager, masseur etc....and I have the certificates to prove it. I think Mrs Wu accepts

BILL

Mr China Person's Message to Me

1. Beware of Chinamen bearing baijiu and cigarettes.
2. Anyone seen to obey any traffic laws will be prosecuted.
3. Because a humble administrator of some dim and distant dynasty got his tang [2nd tone] mixed up with his tang [1st tone], soup has ever since been served as the last course in a Chinese meal.
4. Albert Einstein and Isaac Newton never saw bicycles in China.
5. All translations of England in China is transparent and discipline.
6. The stall holder knows he has got a bargain when the ex-pat thinks he has got one.
7. No job is so small that it need be done by only one person.

8. The number of farmers who discovered The Terracotta Army is in direct proportion to the number of tourists wishing to purchase an authorized, autographed guide book personally signed by the discoverers.

9. Building site : This is a hard hat, soft shoe area.

Well after that, the plagiarist devil inside me thinks I should send a message to Mr China Person. I have long liked the operettas of Gilbert and Sullivan—not to everyone's taste I know—but I believe Gilbert's word skills coupled with Sullivan's music which has many insider jokes for the knowledgeable musician—are really appealing and deserve more serious consideration. When, perhaps I should say "if", I retire I want to write a Chinese version of their operetta, The Mikado. Here's some offerings to date you can sing along to with the tunes. With apologies to G & S for sure! They need working on but it will give you a flavour :-

If you want to know who we are . . . .
We are expats in Shanghai
In many a club and bar
You will find us bye and bye
We find and we feed and fuck
And forget if we've any luck!
Sure each one of us's a schmuk!

And . . . .

If some day it should happen that some victims must be found
We've a fucking great long list, yes a fucking great long list
Of society offenders who might think they're underground—
But we know they do exist and we know where they exist!
There's the whistle-blowers who will rat on how we have designed
Our national one child policy from being undermined,
And artists whose hearts are on the left but whose wallet's on the right
And yet the hand that feeds them they're determined so to bite.
About such lousy liars we don't really give a shite,
So we're sure they'd not be missed. So they're right here on the list!

Officials who the cap_it_alist road still choose to take,
Best prepare for a wake as their lives we're forced to take.
And manu_factur_ers who in brand names still choose to fake,
Their lives we'll have to take so their wills they'd better make.
And the wives of party members who quite clearly can't behave
But resort sometimes to murder for their faces just to save.
And those who are in the top hundred rich in PRC

But haven't paid what they should to our Communist Party,
And the one who on Mao Marxist Leninism will insist
I see him on the list, next to others on our list.

And . . . .

Three lady workers here you see
Fresh from The Den Bar hostelry
Seeking out male company
Three lady workers we.
All that you'll get is what you see,
No male is safe we guarantee
The evening's young and we're easy
Three lady workers we.
Three Chinese maids, all males be wary
We don't come from no seminary,
All we will say is, *Hello, Dearie,*
Buy us a drink and score
[What d' you expect from a whore!]

Yes, there's a heap of work to be done on it but I'll
get round to it when I've time and it will all be tongue
in cheek, believe me, because I cannot understand anyone
who comes to visit or work in China and who does not
come to love the place. It's just . . . . well as I said at the
beginning, I just love it!

FU

L over come back to me. I hope you are reading that not in the imperative mood but more in what I might call the Afro-Caribbean mood i.e. where the auxiliary (*has* in this case making it the perfect tense) is understood. (It's the way they talk, in case you hadn't noticed.) A kind of enthymematic order. Yes, he's coming back . . . . if not to me, at least to Shanghai and that's good enough for me. Once he's on home territory he's mine, trust me. Hark at me! Calling Shanghai my home now—even though I haven't got a hukou to work here!

He's actually been appointed to a top job. Chief Education Officer in an organisation which calls itself The Shelley Group. It deals in education primarily though social services and the likes are linked to it. He's obviously the right man for the educational part of the business with the experience he's recently had in Beijing and Mongolia not to mention his time in Shanghai. Even advises local Chinese schools on international courses now so he must be getting and he must have some guanxi!

It's odd, though, isn't it, that an education group should name itself after such a crazy poet? Shelley actually got kicked out of Oxford so I read so it's hardly appropriate to name an educational institution after him, is it? A failed, unwanted student? Well, there is the revolutionary side to his character and maybe that has a kind of retro 60s appeal here in China? And I expect in some ways Chinese education is going through a bit of a revolution with the ever increasing numbers of high school students opting to follow international courses and then study abroad. Chinese brain drain in the 21st century? Well, what's in a name, anyway? That which we call a rose . . . .

He doesn't actually start here until August but I have managed to get him some part time business which means he can take some time out here in the interim. I've been asked, along with others, to write some blurb about my work in China for a government publication which will be printed and disseminated soon. Supposedly it's to give the international community here and abroad a picture of the real, modern China and not the clap trap they get in a lot of literature that's been turned out by the disaffected minority or expatriates who have just come to rubbish our achievements. People who bite the hand that feeds them! (Oh, yes, I have my contacts and my guanxi too! Well, in my line of work . . . .) So I informed the appropriate Government appointee and told her I had a friend (nudge,

nudge, wink, wink) who, though he was useless in terms of speaking Mandarin, was an expert—Oxbridge graduate and all that—in English language and literature and could turn the Chinglish churned out by translating robots no better than Google translations in Beijing into the real, colloquial McCoy thereby making the publication instantly readable and getting it a wider audience. You know the sort of thing : changing, *Vacate the thoroughfare, my man* to *Get out the fucking way, arsehole*! Mind you I don't know what he would make of *Populace Direct Bus Glasses Supermarket* and *Prohibit playing Kongming latent we are all safe* . . . . I'm sure he'll manage though! She liked the idea and so, Bob's your uncle. But, how, you might well ask does he do this work in Shanghai rather than in the political capital of our masters? Well, he's going to come here in August, he's worked here before and feels quite comfortable here, wants to get back into the swing of things . . . . so why not? After all, he's getting it all on email and downloading it. The beauties of modern technology. She doesn't care as long as the work gets done to the schedule and he'll do that OK . . . . and I promise not to distract him. Well, at least not too often anyway. So he turns up here every so often much to my (and his) delectation and delight.

The wheel, as they say has come full circle. So everything for me is on the up and up again. And so it is for my friends. You'll recall I came here a few years back with Annie, my classmate. Well, she's married an Italian boyfriend and, from what I hear, they live happily ever after in Florence and they have a two year old son, Giovanni. Amazing, really. Annie struggled to speak English so how's she managed Italian, or should I say if she's managed Italian, I really don't know. But with those Mediterranean types it's all emotional gestures most of the time and Annie was good at those I can tell you. Taught me a thing or two in that respect. So I guess that is what has helped her make out. Maybe I ought to try to go and see her sometime! Eleanor is back in business (enough said!) but has, thankfully, kicked that nasty habit of hers which gave her the holiday of a lifetime she really didn't want! It's nice to see her again . . . . occasionally : and I really do see her only occasionally. She's a very busy lady : making up for lost time, I think. Mrs Wu? I suppose you have heard from and know all about. She and her husband are a shining example that if you are prepared work hard you can get good jobs and remuneration in this great country of ours and you can climb up the social ladder. Not to mention your family will do you proud—her daughter has done ever so well! (No little thanks to my Mr Harding—John to me!)

There's some great songs now that sum up my mood nowadays . . . . *I can see clearly now the rain has gone, Top of The World* . . . . you know the kind of thing. Must go to the karaoke and have a sing song and celebrate! Get some of my friends together.

By the way .... You can decide for yourselves what I'm an example of. Am I Thomas Hardy's happily ruined maid or, like Charlene, am I bitter from the sweet? Your call. As if I care!

Bye, bye! Cheerio. Arrivederci! Ciao, straniero bello! Auf Weidersein! Au revoir or should I say A bientot? Let's just stick to Zie Jian .... or Mentian Jian?

From : Wen Jiabao
Premier
Zhongnanhai
Beijing
People's Republic of China

Dear Munna/Balram Halwai/Ashok Sharma and Vale, Valete (i.e. Zie Jian!) dear readers(s)

I hope you have enjoyed getting this snapshot of modern China. Of course, it is a limited one and does not include members of our millionaire/billionaire class (more per head of population than anywhere else in the world even given our 1.3billion population!) who drive around the cities in their Bentleys, Rolls Royces (we have more of them here now than in America!), Masseratis and DB5s or whatever—oh, yes, there's a smart showroom for those in Nanjing Road, Shanghai. Nor, of course, does it give you a picture of rural life i.e. peasants' ville but at the time of writing the number of inhabitants in the cities actually outnumber those in the rural areas. Have we, or have we not, raised more people out of poverty than in any other part of the world in the last quarter century? However, we are aware (a) that we have to bring more education to peasants' ville and (b) that having secured a good standard of living on our Eastern seaboard and Southern cities we now need to drive the financial investment westwards towards Chengdu, Xian, Tianshui and even Chongqing etc. That is already happening and I am sure you have picked up from these narratives how quickly things get done in China. You have a saying, Rome wasn't built in a day, but then we Chinese weren't part of that project. More's the pity.

As you have noticed we have allowed Bill's message to Mr China Person to be included and have not edited it out as some might think we would have despite its scurrilous content. This proves we are not as censorious as you would believe. Rather we are an open and harmonious society and have nothing to hide. So it is onwards and upwards with us as always.

Well, I do hope you will now consider coming to visit us in China. Yes, this is a tourist plug of course and why not? I can assure you of a great time and the chance to see and visit many places of interest in many different cities in our vast country. And who knows, you may even get a chance to meet one of our contributors (except for Peter that is as he's otherwise engaged, or perhaps I should say detained, at present) as they will be signing copies of the book in nominated book stores* in the main cities. (*These do not include the Bookworm in Sanlitun, Beijing or in Chengdu.) I have also been told to let you know that the editor of this volume (he overrates himself when he refers to himself as the author!) an expatriate who has given many distinguished years of educational expertise to the international and Chinese communities mainly in Beijing, Shanghai, Guangzhou and Zhuhai will gladly supply you with an insider's guide to these cities and others if you can prove you have purchased a copy. He has obviously learned the Chinese ways of doing business. He can be contacted on Facebook. However, I would remind you that that is banned in this country—too decadent and far too politically dangerous. However, I am sure you can find out a way . . . .

Our government changes later this year. It will be a smooth transition of course. The status quo will be maintained, naturally. None of this shilly-shallying with projects and legislation etc such as you get after your democratic elections. Continuity and progression are what we believe in. Keeping things on a steady keel. People like to know where they stand : makes them feel more safe and secure. Yes, and we make sure they know exactly where they stand. We are, after all, The Middle Kingdom and we take the middle way : our middle way, that is.

So it's goodbye from them and it's goodbye from me and it's goodbye from Wen Jiabao.

Yours sincerely

Sheng Yapin
(Secretary)